ONCE UPON A FASTBALL

ALSO BY BOB MITCHELL

Match Made in Heaven

*How My Mother Accidentally Tossed Out My Entire
Baseball-Card Collection
(and Other Sports Stories)*

The Tao of Sports

The Heart Has Its Reasons: Reflections on Sports and Life

ONCE UPON
A FASTBALL

Bob Mitchell

KENSINGTON BOOKS
http://www.kensingtonbooks.com

KENSINGTON BOOKS are published by

Kensington Publishing Corp.
850 Third Avenue
New York, NY 10022

All Kensington titles, imprints and distributed lines are available at special quantity discounts for bulk purchases for sales promotion, premiums, fund-raising, educational or institutional use.

Special book excerpts or customized printings can also be created to fit specific needs. For details, write or phone the office of the Kensington Special Sales Manager: Kensington Publishing Corp., 850 Third Avenue, New York, NY 10022. Attn. Special Sales Department. Phone: 1-800-221-2647.

Kensington and the K logo Reg. U.S. Pat. & TM Off.

Library of Congress Control Number: 2008920452
ISBN-13: 978-0-7582-2687-7
ISBN-10: 0-7582-2687-X

First Hardcover Printing: May 2008
10 9 8 7 6 5 4 3 2 1

Printed in the United States of America

To Susan, again, with love.

(Or to put it in baseball terms,
you are my main squeeze of all time.)

Baseball is the only thing besides the paper clip that hasn't changed.
          —Bill Veeck

A hot dog at the ball game beats roast beef at the Ritz.
          —Humphrey Bogart

The art of fiction is dead. Reality has strangled invention. Only the utterly impossible, the inexpressibly fantastic, can ever be plausible again.
          —Red Smith

1

BALL

THE BRAIN OF A BASEBALL FANATIC consists of ten basic structures, each with unique responsibilities: *medulla* (breathing, heartbeat), *pons* (dreaming), *reticular formation* (brain's sentinel), *thalamus* (sensory information), *cerebellum* (bodily movements, equilibrium), *hippocampus* (long-term storage of information), *amygdala* (aggression, sexual behavior), *hypothalamus* (internal equilibrium), *cerebral cortex* (higher cognitive and emotional functions). And, perhaps most important, the little-known *triviata minor,* a tiny compartment that stores information of no seemingly earthly value, like Ted Lepcio's lifetime slugging percentage, what Don Mueller and Donn Clendenon had in common, Bucky Dent's real name, and who pinch-ran for midget Eddie Gaedel.

⚾

Baseball nut Seth Stein slouches in his La-Z-Boy and looks right into the man's eyes.

The man stares back at him with a look that is vacant and listless, gazing at a point six inches above Seth's head, toward a place a zillion miles in the distance.

The man's secondhand face is wizened and sunken and tan, like a battered old catcher's mitt whose pocket has been broken in and darkened through countless innings of abuse.

The man looks terribly bored, which is understandable, since he has been dead now for thirty-three years. He is staring out at Seth from within his baseball card, and his name is Alpha Brazle.

Seth has been studying the picture album of Papa Sol's old baseball cards for nearly an hour. When he reaches Brazle's card, his mind wanders to the first time his grandfather had ever shown it to him.

"Now, Setharoo, this is ol' Al Brazle," Solomon Stein rhapsodizes to his six-year-old grandson, nourishing the baseball passion he has already bequeathed to Seth via the DNA helix. "Nicknamed Alfie or sometimes Cotton. Began his career late in life, at nine and twenty years, as I recall. Pretty fair southpaw, though. Not as good as Grove or Gomez or Hubbell or Ford or Spahn or Koufax or Carlton, of course. But pretty darn fair."

Seth snaps out of it, eyes the card again. A Bowman 1953 beaut. Number 140. Born Loyal, Oklahoma. Died Grand Junction, Colorado. Baseball fanatic Seth Stein recites it by heart, like a catechism. Lifetime record of 97–64. Played all ten years of his career with the same team, the Cardinals. Not like today's million-dollar, free-agent players, Seth thinks, with more than a tinge of melancholy.

He riffles through a few more pages of the album, comes across Pittsburgh Pirates pitcher Murry Dickson's card, stops and cogitates. Good ol' Murry. Always loved the fact that his parents left out the *a* in his first name. The Tom Edison of the mound, they used to call him, because he loved to experiment out there. Stan Musial once cracked that he wouldn't have given his mother anything good to hit. Won twenty in '51, then lost twenty-one in '52. Unreal. Best thing about him was that during the off-season, he was a carpenter, just like Papa Sol.

Seth Stein pauses to give his *triviata minor* a rest. He turns the page, removes a Ray Jablonski Topps card from its four rococo cardboard pasties (one for each corner) that are attached with LePage's Gripspreader Mucilage Glue and have been clinging miraculously to the album page since well before he was born. He sniffs the back of the card, aspirating the nearly faded aroma of pink bubble gum powder like Ferdinand the Bull inhaling a flower's fragrance deeply, lustily. The magical smell is still there after all these decades.

Seth returns Ray to his final resting place and flips through more pages, taking affectionate ganders at Coot Veal and Cot Deal, Duane Pillette and Howie Pollett, Turk Lown, Sam Jethroe, Herm Wehmeier, Bud Podbielan, Roy Smalley, Johnny Klippstein, Johnny Wyrostek, Matt Batts (*Matt Batts!*), Dave Jolly, Virgil Jester (what a pair of clowns), Solly Hemus, Wayne Terwilliger, Ned Garver (how'd he ever win twenty games for the '51 Browns, who lost 102?), Gus Zernial, Al Zarilla, Reno Bertoia, Granny Hamner, Dee Fondy, Eddie Yost ("the Walking Man"), Eddie Waitkus (shot in a hotel room with a rifle by a deranged female fan), Vinegar Bend Mizell.

Oh baby.

All these gentlemen are fossils frozen in time, ossified in their fake poses. The shell-shocked Brazle poses goofily with arms above head, ball in glove and left hand gripping it, preparing for the curve he will never throw. Boston Braves utility man Sibby Sisti assumes a silly, stiff crouch, with left gloved hand on left knee and bare right hand on right knee, as if to conduct some bizarre self-examination of his patellae. Philadelphia Athletics first sacker Ferris Fain smiles straight ahead as he stretches out his right gloved hand to reach, perilously, for a ball coming from a totally different direction from where the camera apparently is.

Seth closes the album and his eyes. The rectangular $3\frac{1}{2}$ x $2\frac{1}{2}$-inch cardboard surfaces with frozen men peering out are mirrors to his soul, reflecting who he was, who he is, who he will become.

He is thinking about these frozen men, not as ballplayers, but as human beings. What ever became of them? After their fifteen minutes of fame, what did they make of their lives? Did they go downhill from there or find peace of mind and happiness?

He is thinking about what these players were like when they reached the age of thirty-three, like he himself just did today, October 19, 2006. (Baseball historian Seth Stein notes that an astounding percentage of these men actually retired at this very age, or thereabouts.) Did these guys end up accomplishing in other ways? Or did they proceed to fall from memorable icons on baseball cards to forgettable ne'er-do-wells? Did they become a U.S. senator, like Jim Bunning, or a disgruntled, paranoid night watchman who died in misery, like Carl Furillo?

He is thinking about where he is now in his own life, approaching a midpoint marker going back to the Bible (Psalms 90:10). *Nel mezzo del cammin,* as Dante put it, smack in the middle of our seventy-year journey.

Like the men in the cards, his life has had a past, a present, and a future. He is thinking about all he has accomplished: a Ph.D. at age twenty-four, his appointment to the Harvard faculty, the five published books. And all he has endured: the failed marriage to and painful divorce from the petulant Julie, the heart disease and recent quadruple bypass surgery, the loss of his parents early on, the loss of his Papa Sol. He is thinking about all he is involved with now: the book he is writing; the stimulating freshman seminar he's teaching; spending time with his beloved Grandma Elsie; watching his son, Sammy, grow up to be a man; his stupendous girlfriend, Kate.

Most of all, Seth is thinking about what will become of him. About the ponderous issues of mortality and achievement and relationships. Will he live to see Sammy grow up and get married and make him a grandfather? Will he finish writing the book? Will he even get to watch another World Series? Will he dare to try marriage again? But these questions are sardines compared to this whale of an enigma: Will he ever be able to figure out the mystery of his Papa Sol's sudden disappearance, two years ago, from the face of the earth?

☾

Seth Stein, Associate Professor of History at Harvard, is in the feverish process of gestating his sixth book, *That Which Has Been No Longer Is: Can We Ever Know History?* And while he really loves his Martin acoustic guitar, his Balvenie single-malt Scotch, his feisty squash matches with best friend, Gordon, and of course Sammy, Grandma Elsie, and Kate, he loves History—just as he adores baseball—in quite a different way. More proprietarily. Like the way a dog loves his bone. Meeting the challenge of attempting to "know" the past, to resurrect it in all its glory—not just names, dates, and events, but virtually everything in the air that drives people to action—has become for him a marrow-sucking obsession.

So much so that nearly every one of the ten million available neurons in his gray matter (excluding, of course, the very considerable number dedicated to baseball trivia) is preoccupied with the minutiae of things past: battles, paintings, symphonies, poems, natural disasters, working conditions, biology, technology, meteorology, genealogy . . . A walking encyclopedia, his students call him, those earnest, bushy-tailed freshmen in the *Fundamental Problems of History* seminar he's teaching this term. Flattering, he thinks, but to his mind, most of the credit—genetic and pedagogical—for his extraordinary gift and his passion for History belongs to his teacher, mentor, role model, confidant, and pal, his beloved Papa Sol.

It all began with the bedtime stories.

Stories lovingly concocted by Solomon Stein, then recited at dusk to his four-year-old grandson, whose deep brown eyes sparkle and widen, peeking over the covers, Kilroy-like, as his grandpa's deep, mellifluent voice spins those swashbucklers of times gone by, his majestic baritone meticulously caressing each syllable.

Stories like "The Secret Treasure of the Sierra Padre," "The Puzzling Case of Luiz, King of Barataria," and "The Adventures of Jean Lamain, Pirate of the Azores."

. . . and suddenly, from out of nowhere, Jean Lamain, the handsome, brave, audacious, one and only Jean Lamain, outlaw of the Seven Seas, takes his trusty sword, Geneviève, out of her scabbard and, with one skillful flick of his wrist . . .

Seth is officially hooked on the Past.

As he grows older, the mentoring continues, with Papa Sol donating many a tender evening reading historical novels to the ever-rapt Seth: *Ivanhoe, Kidnapped, Quo Vadis, A Tale of Two Cities, The Count of Monte Cristo.* Seth's favorite visits to the past, though, are the tales of Greek mythology.

Solomon Stein's powerful carpenter's hands cradle the entranced Seth on one side of him and Frances Ellis Sabin's *Classical Myths That Live Today* on the other, narrating to the lad the exploits of gods and goddesses and heroes and heroines: the Twelve Labors of Hercules, Apollo and Cassandra, Athena's birth from Zeus's forehead, Atalanta and the golden apples, the fall of Icarus, Sisyphus and his rock, Daphne and her laurel tree, Perseus and Medusa, Theseus and the Minotaur, Hector and Achilles, Odysseus and Polyphemus.

Young Seth looks up at his Papa Sol, smiles at *his* hero, shuts his eyes. With Solomon Stein's voice urging him on, he rockets himself miraculously back to those olden times. Mounted on the back of the wingèd steed Pegasus, he glides across the diamond-studded nocturnal sky, Cheshire grin pasted on his cherubic puss. He is actually *living* way back when!

◖◗

Seth settles behind the wheel of Jezebel, his doddering but dependable 1983 Buick Skylark, en route to Grandma Elsie's house on the other side of Cambridge.

Jezebel knows the way to Grandma's house so well that, except for moral support, she barely needs Seth at the wheel. Wobbling along Cambridge Street, hobbling past Harvard Yard, Harvard Square, and Cambridge Common, she splutters up Brattle Street, sputters past Mount Auburn Hospital and Fresh Pond. Right at the fork onto Belmont, another right onto Cushing, and after a few more rights, she staggers to her destination, grinding to an exhausted halt and relieved to find repose at her familiar spot in the middle of the crack-filled, grass-sprouted driveway. Oil drips from under her hood and onto the pavement, like so many beads of sweat.

Seth exits Jeze, gives her an affectionate pat, and wistfully surveys the grizzled, gray-shingled house of Elsie Adler Stein. Funny how you can look at this house a thousand times, he thinks, and each time, a new memory emerges from behind its cobwebs.

Glancing down at the sidewalk in front of the house, Seth revisits with vivid clarity that special cloud-covered, bone-rattling Saturday morn eons ago, when Papa Sol is guiding him on his little red Schwinn, its training wheels amputated, like a grandfather red-tailed hawk coaxing his grandchick to the edge of the cliff, then letting him go on his own, for the first time, his feet pedaling cautiously, then more confidently, his little boy's innocent cackles of avian joy celebrating the realization of his first successful solo flight. Grandma hawk Elsie cackles, too, from the porch swing, between sips of chamomile tea.

His eyes pan to the mailbox Solomon Stein had built over twenty years ago. The house-shaped box is carved out of redwood, its battered body painted a peppy scarlet, its roof a stern navy. The door is a baseball, white with crimson stitching. In place of a red flag on the side, Papa Sol had fashioned a plywood structure depicting two overlapping fat red woolen socks, with white toes and heels. Up above, some twenty feet in the air and attached to the main mailbox by a wooden dowel, a smaller replica of the house below teeters, swaying in the autumn breeze, the word AIRMAIL scrawled across a wooden sign fastened to the top of its roof.

Solomon and Elsie Stein had shared this old house for twenty-four joyful years, ever since they moved to Cambridge from Berkeley. Baseball nut Sol had moved himself and Elsie around according to the object of his passion: first to New York, in 1951, to be close to his beloved Giants; then, he followed the Jints to San Francisco when the team relocated there in '58; and finally, when the club became virtually hopeless in '80 (fifth place, seventeen games behind), he finally tossed his hands up, and up and moved to Cambridge, heavyheartedly switching his allegiances to the lovable and long-suffering Red Sox.

Aside from Sol and Elsie's house in Berkeley and his present Cambridge town house, Seth has occupied no other domicile than this one, at least none he can recall. When he was three, one frigid winter night, Elsie had announced to him the tragic news, which entered his unsuspecting ears as so much gibberish, between her sobs and his toddler's capacity to comprehend.

"Mommy . . . Daddy . . . airplane . . . down . . . heaven . . . never . . . see them . . . *dahlink* . . . my baby!"

◖C◗

"Honey, I'm home!" Seth singsongs playfully to his grandma as he ascends the thirteen creaky stairs on the way to her second-floor bedroom.

Nothing.

"Bubby, it's me!" he insists, concerned about Grandma Elsie's unaccustomed silence, negotiating the steps two at a clip.

When Seth enters the bedroom and sees Elsie's seventy-seven-year-old face peeking out from under the covers, all the blood drains from his. In fact, the face he now observes appears not to be Elsie's at all, but Eve's, in Masaccio's unsettling 1427 fresco, *The Expulsion from Paradise:* the sunken eyes, the mouth agape, the confusion and the shame.

Seth misses her beaming countenance, the one she'd worn sempiternally before Papa Sol mysteriously disappeared two years ago without a trace. He misses her smiling face that usually greets him on his frequent visits, the smile that is radiant, solar. He misses her spry, mischievous demeanor that, through the years, has earned her his pet nickname, "Grandma Elfie." But the not knowing why and the nagging questions surrounding her beloved husband have, on this occasion, robbed her of the frivolity and energy she exhibits on good days.

Today, apparently, isn't one.

A single tear meanders down Elsie's pale cheek, and Seth knows she's been thinking of Sol. He has come prepared and offers a Kleenex.

Holding her hand tenderly, he peruses the dressing table, which is cluttered with History. The sepia photo of Sol and Elsie on their honeymoon in Lake George, summer of '46: They are on the porch of some country inn, seated on a swing, gazing into each other's eyes, oblivious to the Kodak Brownie camera that is capturing their image. The black-and-white photo of Seth's now-deceased parents, Simon and Rebecca, a woeful surrogate for authentic memories, but still comforting to Seth every time his eyes devour its details. The color photo of Papa Sol and his ballplayer hero, Willie Mays, their arms around each other's waists, Sol's smile improbably wider than the Say Hey Kid's. The polished oak jewelry box Sol had carved for Elsie for their fiftieth wedding anniversary, with those delicate, painstakingly fashioned flowers that were his artisan's signature.

Seth looks down at Elsie, this proud, independent woman whose mostly joyous life has had its share of sunshine: loving husband, doting son and grandson and great-grandson, selfless community service through her teaching and charity work. Her spouse's recent vanishing being the only dark cloud still shrouding all these rays of happiness.

Seth is hoping that Elsie's sunny essence will ultimately burn off the cloud and that in the end, when it's her time, she will shuffle off this mortal coil in peace and serenity, as in one of those diaphanous and breathlessly gorgeous cinematic scenes featuring Greer Garson or Loretta Young.

Elsie moves her head toward him, and Seth senses that she has something urgent to communicate. Her voice, usually so jolly and resonant, is today reduced to a barely audible susurrus.

"Happy Birthday, *bubeleh*," she says weakly but with grace. "So, you *alter kocker*, you finally made it to the big three-three. *Mazel tov!*

"Top drawer," she whispers, gesturing toward the night table. "For you, my *dahlink*."

"For *me*, bubby?"

Seth opens the top drawer and removes from it a square package wrapped in crinkled brown paper. A yellowed envelope taped on top reads, in Papa Sol's strong master carpenter's hand: *For Setharoo. With love, Papa Sol.*

A lump forms in Seth Stein's throat. No one but his Papa Sol ever called him Setharoo.

"I found this one day in his drawer," Elsie says, her voice crackling, a second tear forming in the corner of her left eye. "Until now, I kept hoping your Papa Sol would return and give it to you personally."

Elsie helps herself to another tissue. "I still can't believe he disappeared without a word. I mean, after fifty-eight beautiful years of marriage, no warning, no good-byes, just *poof!*"

Elsie's words catapult Seth back into the unremitting quandary that has gnawed at him for the past two years:

How could his hero, his pal, his role model—this amazing, upbeat, inspiring grandfather, father figure, and human being—have simply vanished? How could a man so beloved by his wife and his grandson and his great-grandson not have at least had the decency to speak to them, to let them know his reasons for leaving? If some tragic accident had befallen him, surely they would have been informed by the authorities.

And if this was a simple case of disappearance and change of identity . . . then *why?* Sol had given neither Elsie nor Seth the vaguest hint of unhappiness or dissatisfaction. Only love, affection, kindness, and sacrifice. An unsolved mystery that has left them both brokenhearted, devastated, starving for the truth.

"I know, I know, Elfie," Seth says. "Just *poof!*" Seth injects the harrowing word with a dose of onomatopoeic fun by puffing out his cheeks, expelling the four letters into the air through his protruded lips, and emitting a high-pitched, comical yelp. It is the kind of facial gesture and sound effect that Elsie has herself used to cheer up Seth all these years.

Seth's performance elicits a hint of the old elfin Elsie, and her smile floods the bedroom.

But not for long. Grandma Elsie looks up at her flesh and blood with weary eyes red and filmy from today's frustration and sadness. They are the eyes of a prizefighter that are searing into the soul of a referee who has stopped the fight for no apparent reason, begging him for answers.

"You need to rest, bubby," Seth says. "Shall I open the package now?"

"No, *dahlink.* This is between you and your Papa Sol. Take it home with you and open it up when it feels right. I'm sure that's the way he would've wanted it."

Elfie closes her eyes and ekes out a smile just as Seth plants a life-confirming kiss on her right cheek.

(C)

On the drive home, Seth's brain is engorged with questions. How long can Grandma go on like this? Why did Papa Sol do this to her? Why did he do this to *me*? Did something terrible happen to him? And if not, where *is* he now? Did he take his own life? If so, what did he withhold from us that was making him miserable enough to do that? What could he have left me in that package?

Damn you, Papa Sol! I miss you, Papa Sol!

Jeze is still sweating oil as she limps to and plops herself down at her spot at the curb on Harvard Street, in front of Seth's town house. Gotta get that leak fixed one of these days, he mutters as he inserts the key in the door.

In his study, Seth tosses his yellow-and-navy parka and trusty Red Sox cap on the floor and pours himself a generous Balvenie. Rocks (three), twist, half splash of soda. Just like Papa Sol had taught him after his high school graduation. An essential rite of passage, this Scotch thing. Sol's drink of preference, then Seth's. One of many treasured batons passed on from grandfather to grandson.

Nothing like a Balvenie before dinner to excite the palate. To prepare the appetite. Mostly, to unjangle the nerves and calm the psyche. Been a long day for Seth, between a tight morning squash match he'd lost to best pal Gordon Stewart (15–13 in the mind-numbing fifth), all that work on the final structuring of his book and the gestation of that nettlesome opening chapter "In Search of Lost Time," the minor quarrel he'd had with sweetheart Kate, the bittersweet visit with Elsie.

Oozing into his chocolate-colored Naugahyde La-Z-

Boy, he takes his first sip of the single-malt elixir he has grown to relish, ever since Sol had introduced him to it and educated him about its vast superiority to "ordinary" Scotch whisky. *Ah, that first sip!* Producing rapture on the approximate order of that first prebreakfast sip of joe and that first postdinner puff on a Cohiba Esplendidos (another baton passed to him by Papa Sol).

As the Balvenie slides down his throat, both shocking and soothing his system, he squeezes his lips together tight until they disappear completely, exposing his top six front teeth, and scrunches up both cheeks until they hurt—just the way Bogie does whenever he has a belt onscreen.

The study is so Seth: *Tornado* would best describe it. Squash racquets and sneakers here, guitar there (a Martin 000-28EC), in every cranny pages filled with names, places, dates, data—typed and with copious marginal notes that are handwritten in red uni-ball. Word puzzle books, thesauri, dictionaries, foreign dictionaries, dictionaries of slang and of etymology and of synonyms and of cultural literacy. But mostly history books, some his own and some withdrawn from Widener Memorial Library, wall to wall and floor to ceiling: thrown pell-mell on shelves between cinder blocks, piled up in untidy stacks on the floor, strewn in random clumps across his large Solomon Stein–built cherry desk.

Spread on the surface of a small oak table in one corner of the study is a chaotic yet artful still life of baseball bric-a-brac that would have made Cézanne mighty proud. Encyclopedias, old yearbooks and game programs, yellowed newspaper clippings. A Rawlings PM1 glove that had been Papa Sol's in the fifties. A black-and-white photo of Bobby Thomson's famous home run from the deciding '51 pennant game, the ball frozen in midflight, inside a simple black metal frame. A group photo of the 2004 World Champion Boston Red Sox. And the most special bric of all, an old baseball encased in Plexiglas, the one Papa Sol caught off the bat of Giants second baseman Davey Williams on June 28, 1954. Charity game against the Bosox. Leo Kiely on the mound vs. the Giants' Paul Giel. The home run hitting contest between the Say Hey Kid and the Splendid Splinter before the first pitch. A game Papa Sol recounted to Seth frequently at bedtime, and especially how he plucked Davey's foul out of thin air with his strong carpenter's right hand.

The pungent odor that pervades the room and makes it uniquely Seth's suggests somewhere between a library and a locker room.

He takes a second lingering sip of his Balvenie and examines first the package Papa Sol has left for him, then the yellowed envelope. Feels slightly catatonic, not from the Scotch, but from the shock of being face to face with the two bequests. As if his grandfather were right there with him once more, poised to speak.

A third sip, and he is finally in the frame of mind to open the envelope. Slowly and with care. After all, this is *History,* the past brought to life. In an instant, Sol will be speaking to him from a place and a time that are not here and not now.

Seth withdraws from the envelope a yellowed page. The words on it are written neatly, in Papa Sol's virile hand, stacked in irregular lines that look, curiously, like the right half of Vulcan's anvil and read like a vers libre poem. He enunciates the lyrical words, one at a time and aloud, chanting them as they trip, one after the other, off his tongue:

My dearest Sylvan one,
My spirit hears nothing if not ditties of no tone.
My forehead burns, my tongue is parched.
Can a soul ever return from the silent streets of a
    little town?
Your legacy is in the Attic.
That is all you need to know.
With all my love, Your Papa Sol.
P.S. What will you do after the ball?

Huh?

Seth reads the note again, even more deliberately. Then a third time. He takes another sip, cradling his chin between left thumb and forefinger.

Huh?

Reading it once more, appreciating the beauty of the words but still clueless as to their meaning, Seth searches for answers, line by line.

Why "Sylvan"? Why the capital *S*? Why compare me to a forest?

Why the negativity? (Papa Sol was generally so upbeat.) *"Ditties of no tone"*?

Was Papa Sol very sick, without anyone's knowing it? Stranded on a desert island?

He always lived in a city—New York, San Francisco, Boston. So why the reference to the "little town"? Did he ever spend time in one?

Legacy? In the Attic? Gotta go look in Grandma's attic in the morning . . .

"All you need to know"? Why the throwaway line?

"After the ball"?

Papa Sol used to fall asleep in his favorite easy chair, holding some volume of poetry or another against his chest, Seth recalls. True, he was in fact a poet, in the way he lived life and in his carpentry. Used to call himself "the Bard of Wood." Maybe that explains the form of the note. But why such dense poetic language? Why the secrecy? Did Papa Sol, as he often used to do, want to push me to the limit, to egg me on, to encourage me to figure things out for myself, to struggle through difficulty in order to attain goals? *Per aspera ad astra,* Papa Sol used to spout. "To the stars through adversity."

Sol's note also awakens within Seth the cherished memory of those challenging word games his grandfather used to play with him and that he grew to love: poetry writing, puzzles, etymological searches, secret codes, palindromes and anagrams, linguistic brainteasers.

An ache fills Seth's head, a dull pounding, the relentless hammer in the old Anacin commercial. Conflicting feelings of resentment at Sol's disappearance and love for his lost mentor swirl around and through his cerebral creases.

But back to the note. Reminds him of the Latin passages he used to have to translate in high school, from Vergil or Ovid perhaps, the sense of which always seemed obfuscated at first, by the strangeness of the words and the weird syntax. But he always managed to figure out the meaning, by dint of perseverance and the use of both his left and right brains.

Seth is feeling bone weary, the Balvenie is beginning to take effect, his desire to decode Papa Sol's cryptic note is being trumped by his curiosity to discover the contents of the package.

Gingerly, he opens the brown paper wrapping.

Emerging from it, like Venus rising from the sea foam and every bit as lovely, is a square wooden box.

Seth caresses its sensuous surface with his fingertips, as

if the wood were the soft, warm belly of Aphrodite herself. The box is dark brown, probably some kind of oak, perhaps mahogany. It is, beyond a doubt, a Solomon Stein. You could always recognize one by its intricate floral patterns and by the distinctive delicacy of the craftsmanship.

The image of Papa Sol's hands appears before Seth's eyes. With most people, you tend to remember a facial characteristic—hair or eyes or nose or lips or smile, maybe a subtle physical deformity. With Sol, it was the hands. They always reminded Seth of the hands of Michelangelo's *David*. Powerful and slightly too large for his body, yet delicate and expressive. Strange, Seth never actually saw his grandfather in the act of chiseling or gouging or filing. One of Sol's peculiar idiosyncrasies. But he could imagine how those mighty hands were capable of fashioning delicate objects of such extraordinary splendor.

Superseding Sol's hands is the vision of a statue of the lovely Pandora—the one from the Greek mythology book Papa Sol used to read to him—clad in toga and sandals, and holding in her hands, chest high, her infamous box.

What would *Sol's* box unleash?

The moment has arrived, and Seth opens the wooden box with caution. The hinged top concludes its 180-degree backward trajectory, revealing a round pale yellow leather object, nestled in its custom-made, green-felt niche. It is a baseball.

Excuse me?

Happily, Seth has a drink nearby.

He takes a languorous sip of Balvenie, considers the ball. Why did Sol leave him a baseball? Why this particular one? Did the note have anything to do with it? The P.S.?

He scours the ball for clues. First thing he notices is the stamped writing, faded and barely legible:

Official
National*League
Ford C. Frick Pres.

Then, under the crimson herringbone stitching:

THE CUSHIONED CORK CENT
Marca Registr

SPALDI

The letters that are missing at the end of these last three
lines—which he assumes to be "ER," "ADA," and "**NG**"—
have become part of a palimpsest, as they are obscured by
a nasty one-inch-long, one-half-inch-thick blackish scuff
mark, draped horizontally across the surface of the baseball, the ball's personal badge of honor spreading itself out
like some proud eye patch announcing, "I have suffered."
The scuff mark, Seth presumes, is the result of violent contact with a bat. *Very* violent, he deduces, as on closer inspection, he observes a number of tiny shreds of leather
that have grafted themselves onto the ebony laceration,
like scar tissue coalescing to cover over a wound.

The ball looks to be pure horsehide, but to be certain
of its authenticity, he counts the stitches. Yep, 108 of those
red beauties, consistent with MLB standards.

Okay, so Papa Sol obtained a ball that was hit very hard
at a National League game. He must've gotten more than a
few in his time, so why leave me this one?

He has seen hundreds of baseballs, no, probably thou-
sands, up close. Balls Sol and he had had catches with,
balls Sol had hit fungo to him with, balls he'd hit and
pitched and fielded with his pals in Little League, balls

he'd seen during BP at Candlestick and Fenway. But *this* one seems special, for some reason, and not just because it was left to him by Papa Sol. Just something about it.

Seth puts on his historian's Sherlock Holmes cap and invokes his encyclopedic reservoir of baseball knowledge. Let's see, Ford Frick was president of the NL from . . . 1935 to 1951, the year in which he became commissioner of Major League Baseball and ceded his NL presidency to . . . Warren Giles. Ergo, Papa Sol had to have been between the ages of seven and twenty-three (he was born in 1928) when he somehow acquired the hard-hit baseball at some National League game.

Okay, so exactly *where and when and how did he acquire it?*

Seth is stuck, unable to deduce anymore. From the trying day, the Balvenie, and now this.

He finishes his drink, sucks an ice cube into his mouth, chomps on it, takes another gander at the ball. So much to absorb. First the note, then the ball. What does it all mean? How Papa Sol loved baseball! How he passed on his passion to me! Papa Sol, I *miss* you! So why the hell did you leave this ball for me?

Why?

Seth touches the ball for the first time, rotates it with his fingertips, allows it to settle in his palm, and the room begins to spin, nearly imperceptibly at first. Is it the Balvenie? He looks even more intently at the ball, as though by staring it down, he could somehow unlock the secret it holds, could listen to what Sol is trying to tell him from some different, distant place and time.

The spinning accelerates. Can't be the Balvenie. Only had one.

What is this, a dream? A nightmare? A hallucination? A tale straight out of Poe? H. G. Wells? Kafka?

Faster and faster the room turns, clockwise. Seth takes a deep, self-preserving ujjai breath, tries to hang on. Sheesh. Am I having a stroke? Another coronary infarction?

He takes his pulse, it seems normal. Phew.

The rotation of the spinning tightens, narrows, and Seth feels like he is going down—could it be?—*the rabbit hole*. Curiouser and curiouser.

No, it is more like being in the eye of a tornado: calm inside, swirling outside. He hears a strain of music within the turbulent vortex, the same music that is playing while Dorothy is being transported via tornado to Oz. *Dah-de-lah-de-lah.* But he didn't get bumped on the head, like Dorothy did. And he didn't munch on a madeleine infused in linden tea, either, like Marcel in Proust's opus. So what was the genesis of this upheaval?

Could it be . . . Papa Sol's baseball?

In the midst of the chaos, Seth is no longer feeling panic, but a sudden calm. The calm *after* the storm.

Another musical riff starts up, this time, yes, it's from the Beatles' tour de force "A Day in the Life." He knows the song by heart, has studied its place in History. Even knows that this riff, the one that starts low and builds higher and higher and higher in intensity and volume and octaves, occurs twice during the song—between 1:54 and 2:16, then between 3:59 and 4:19.

As the music—itself sounding like a swirling twister—intensifies, building to a fever pitch, so accordingly does the maelstrom's velocity, but oddly the calm inside, where Seth is, remains constant.

Without warning, all around the inside perimeter of the cylinder, rotating counterclockwise past Seth's eyes one by one, like a spectacular, larger-than-life slide show, are people—*figures from History!*—and places, too, from the past.

Good God, there's the invention of the wheel! And Hammurabi and his Code of Laws in Mesopotamia! And Stonehenge being built and King Tut being buried at Thebes and Moses' exodus from Egypt and Alexander the Great and the Great Wall of China and Jesus' crucifixion . . .

First the panic, then the calm, now the ecstasy. Seth is beside himself with joy: He's not sure what's going on, or why, or why him, but surrounded by History itself, he is filled with an inebriating sensation he's never known.

There's Mohammed with the Koran and William the Conqueror at Hastings and the signing of the Magna Carta and Genghis Khan invading China and Columbus setting out on his voyage and Michelangelo on his Sistine scaffold and Martin Luther at Wittenberg and Galileo with his telescope and the Pilgrims landing at Plymouth Rock and Louis XIV at Versailles and Ben Franklin with his bifocals and the signing of the Declaration of Independence. . .

It dawns on him that these people and places from History are appearing in chronological order. From the beginning of a human presence on earth to, well, there's Napoleon at Waterloo, so the tour is at least taking him up to 1815.

Nope, even further. There's Edison with his bulb and Bell with his phone and the Wright Brothers at Kitty Hawk. . .

The Beatles' riff is about to conclude orgasmically in its final burst of a chord.

. . . and Chancellor Hitler speechifying and the crumbling battleships at Pearl Harbor and the atomic bomb mushrooming at Hiroshima and Gandhi's assassination. . .

And the music intensifies even more, almost unbearably now, then ends abruptly, in that rousing, raucous, brash, clashing, strident, high-pitched, piercing, trumpety climax. And the tornado decelerates and grinds to a halt. And Seth is deposited gently on the ground. And he looks around, gawking, his jaw dropped in disbelief.

It is no longer 2006.

2

MIRACLE?

IT IS 1951.

Seth knows it is, because, still gawking, he is standing next to a pile of *New York World-Telegram and Sun*s stacked messily on the ground in front of Hessing's Luncheonette.

The wrinkled page on top tells him it's 1951. As he looks up, the street signs tell him he's standing at the corner of Forty-ninth Street and Thirteenth Avenue.

Dear Lord.

This is where . . . Papa Sol and Grandma Elsie lived in the early days . . . their old neighborhood . . . Borough Park . . . Brooklyn, New York . . . Forty-ninth Street and . . .

You could have knocked him over with an egg cream.

Seth strolls up Thirteenth Avenue, greeting the unknown with a nervous anticipation akin to what Neil Armstrong must have felt when he took his first steps up there.

He didn't notice the exact date in the paper. Must be autumn, though, since virtually every man on the street is wearing an overcoat and a hat. The scene is a monochrome. Same color coats (gray, black, navy, brown), same style hats (fedoras). Like he's stuck in a black-and-white movie or a sepia daguerreotype.

"Those were simpler days, Setharoo," Papa Sol used to tell him while reminiscing about this epoch. "Nothing fancy, nothing hi-tech, just, well, *simpler.*"

Historian Seth is beginning to understand. *My God, I'm actually here. Seeing how Papa Sol lived back then.*

It is early evening. Men walk briskly from workplaces and bus stops and perches at watering holes, eagles heading back to the aerie for a hot, wholesome, home-cooked meal with the wife and chicks.

Ambling up Thirteenth Avenue, Seth is mesmerized by the parked cars, two rows of hippos napping curbside until it is time to awaken and mosey along. They are all curvaceous and corpulent, and you could just about squeeze two of today's compacts into any one of them. Lots of two-tones, loads of chrome. And the huge grilles. Looks like they're all grinning. Especially that Buick over there, the one with the overbite and the eighteen oversize, curved chrome teeth on the grille, and the ship's portholes on the sides. And getta loada those gigantic bumpers and those mammoth, protruding hood ornaments, birds and beasts of every imaginable species. And some models are wearing shades over the tops of their windshields, like the visors worn by those old-time newspapermen.

These behemoths are lined up, single file, only six to a block, one big, gorgeous cartoon tugboat after another. Not a Japanese or Korean or German creation in sight. Yep, every single one of these beached whales is made right here, in the good ol' US of A. And the names—so virile, so adventurous! Packard Patrician. DeSoto Sportsman.

Dodge Wayfarer. Buick Roadmaster. Kaiser-Frazer Vagabond. Nash Statesman. Studebaker Commander. Seth's nose is assaulted by a battery of alien aromas chattering in a crazy, exotic dialect with which he is not conversant. Pungent, spicy whiffs of pastrami and corned beef and stuffed derma emanate from Skilowitz Delicatessen. From Barton's Bonbonniere waft smells of chocolate and nuts: turtles, assorteds, Viennese crunch, truffles, almond bark. From Miller's Appetizing, a confluence of smoked herring in sour cream and schmalz, lox, whitefish, butterfish, and sour and half-sour pickles, bobbing like petite green kayaks in their Brobdingnagian barrels of brine.

Crossing Thirteenth, he doubles back aimlessly past Ebinger's bakery, where his nostrils continue to party, luxuriating in the scents of chocolate seven-layer cakes and blackout cakes and Othellos and huckleberry crumb pies.

He is a stranger in a strange land, an Alex in a topsy-turvy Wonderland where old is new and stale is fresh and past is present and humdrum is extraordinary.

Down the avenue he perambulates. There's Linick's Toys, whose sign flashes red neon letters (the *k* is on the blink) and in whose windows are displayed, by category, comic books with unfamiliar titles: *Buck Jones, Gabby Hayes, Reno Browne, The Durango Kid* ("cowboys"); *Rocket to the Moon, King Solomon's Mines, Mysterious Island, Mystery in Space, Blackhawk* ("mystery and adventure"); *The Crypt of Terror, The Vault of Horror, The Haunt of Fear, Weird Fantasy* ("horror"); and *Tom and Jerry, Pogo, Little Lulu, Nancy & Sluggo, Red Ryder* ("general").

He stops at Markell's to gawk at odd-looking shoes he'd only heard about in song and story. Blue suedes. White bucks. Saddles. Rockabillies. Alligators.

"KA-CHING!" sneezes the green monster of a cash register at the back of the store. So, there *was* life before computers, Seth notes, with a wry smile, as he crosses Thirteenth Avenue again, sauntering back north.

Like the Siren's call to Odysseus's men, a wondrous profusion of notes beckons to him, cascading from the direction of Jaynel's Music, an otherworldly medley of haunting oldies that are brand-new this year: "Be My Love" by Mario Lanza, "Because of You" by Tony Bennett, "If" by Perry Como, "Jezebel" *("Jezebel"!)* by Frankie Lane, "I Apologize" by Billy Eckstine, "Come On-a My House" by Rosemary Clooney, "Tennessee Waltz" by Patti Page.

Seth could easily stay there all evening, nose pressed against glass, but he presses on, impelled by some force he is only vaguely aware of but that, robotlike, he obeys.

There's Moe Penn Haberdasher. *Haberdasher.* Seth falls in love again with that word, a word he hasn't heard since childhood. In the window, the cream of the cream is on display when it comes to *chapeaux de mode*—felt hats, mohair hats, straw hats, you name it. In gray and brown and tan and black and charcoal, with solid bands or two-tone or even plaid, if you prefer. Fedoras mostly, but also homburgs and porkpies and Sinatras and stetsons and boaters and panamas.

Imagine: a store dedicated solely to *hats.*

An obvious historical fact occurs to Seth, but startling nonetheless. No cell phones. People are actually having *live conversations.*

Two men walking just behind are engaged in one, a spirited one at that. They are damn near twins: five feet nine, gray fedoras with plain black bands, full-length charcoal overcoats with black faux-fur lapels.

"Geez, whatta game today, huh? Dem Bums sure showed 'em! What was it, ten nuttin'?"

"Yeah. Hey, you said a mouthful. That guy Labine, he was sure cookin' with gas, y'know?"

"Yep, tossed a dilly, a real humdinger."

Seth is triply intrigued, by the accents, the baseball allusions, the colloquial enthusiasm of the two men. Besides, the historian in him naturally wants to make contact with fellow human beings from this bygone day. He slows down a smidgeon so he can join in.

"Excuse me, fellows, I wonder—"

"An' y'know what? We're gonna win again t'morrow!"

"No doubt about it, my good friend. No doubt about it."

"Pardon me, guys, but I—"

"Yeah, then on to the Yanks, and us Bums'll be woild cham*peens* at last!"

"That'd really be somethin', now wouldn't it?"

"I hate to bother you, gentlemen, but could you—"

"Well, here's my block, pal. Can't keep Helen waitin' tonight. It's salmon croquettes and succotash!"

"OK, kiddo. See ya tomorrow. An' let's go, Bums!"

Seth now realizes: He's here, but he's not here.

Unperturbed by this discovery and still in awe of just *being* here, Seth hangs a right up Forty-ninth Street, feeling like a tourist who's arrived in Paris or Budapest or Addis Ababa for the first time. Everything seems old, but strangely new. There's Al Del Gaudio's barbershop on the right, with the weather-beaten, nicked white horsey and the shiny red fire engine car, both jacked up four feet above the floor, both more than happy to accommodate the next bawling toddler for his or her very first tortured haircut.

He approaches New Utrecht Avenue, with its elevated train track, the West End Line. There's Monte Greenhut's Mobil station on the corner, the two attendants in uniforms and ties and Mobil caps—*helping customers out!*—and the impressive sign with the red Pegasus logo on a white background.

Farther up New Utrecht, at Fifty-first, he passes the Loew's Boro Park movie theater. White plastic, sometimes crooked, occasionally missing letters on its black marquis harbinger a double feature:

> A STRE TCAR NAM D DESIRE   MARLON BR NDO
> TH DAY THE E RTH STO D STIL   MICHA L RENNIE

Seth doubles back and hangs a left at Forty-ninth Street, his pace a tad more urgent now, and there's Dr. Yachnes's house on the right, not far from where he began his odyssey, at Hessing's, at the corner of Thirteenth Avenue. A Geiger counter detecting pay dirt, he freezes in front of number 1270.

1270!

He is standing directly in front of the two-story, red-brick edifice that houses Papa Sol and Grandma Elsie.

Could they actually be home?

A dumbstruck Seth stands transfixed, his purple Chuck Taylor high-tops epoxied to the sidewalk.

He notes, with precision and delight, every detail of the house, this house where Sol and Elsie used to live—*and that they inhabit now.* The brick stoop leading up to the burnt-sienna front door with the gold handle and the gold knocker and the gold numbers *1270.* The modest, manicured, rectangular front lawn stretching out between the low, black wrought-iron fencing and the neat row of juniper bushes. The long, badly cracked concrete driveway to the left.

Seth unglues himself and ventures down the driveway, past the high brown fence and the bakery rooftop on the left, past the length of the redbrick exterior of the house on the right, until he reaches the stand-alone, A-frame-roofed, one-and-a-half-car garage at the end.

He lifts open the heavy metal garage door, behind which his grandfather's two-tone green Hudson Hornet hibernates, the one he'd heard so much about.

Papa Sol must be home.

Seth's hands quaver and his heart lub-dubs as he closes the garage door and approaches the back-door stoop. Forgetting that no one can see or hear him, he tiptoes up the five steps of the pebbled stoop, looks to see if the coast is clear, gently turns the knob of the poorly painted dark brown back door. It opens.

Seth is inside 1270 Forty-ninth Street. *Home of Solomon and Elsie Stein.* To his left is a tiny blue bathroom that contains nothing but a blue porcelain commode, a mirror-faced medicine cabinet, and a blue porcelain sink with a pristine bar of Lava Soap reposing peacefully in its clear plastic dish.

He hangs two quick rights, and he is in the kitchen. Spick-and-span, not a crumb or a dust bunny to be seen. That Elsie, always so neat. On the kitchen table are a *New York Herald Tribune* dated October 2, 1951, a box of Wheaties with a picture of Pirates slugger Ralph Kiner on the front, three place settings for breakfast, and three chairs.

Seth continues his silent tour, turning right again after the steep, sixteen-step northbound staircase, and enters a rectangular study area.

Official Museum of the Early Fifties.

Recently purchased hardcover books are strewn on a black-and-white, faux veined marble coffee table: Herman Wouk's *The Caine Mutiny,* James Jones's *From Here to Eternity,* Thor Heyerdahl's *Kon-Tiki,* Rachel Carson's *The Sea Around Us,* J. D. Salinger's *The Catcher in the Rye.* Atop Wouk's novel sits a letter addressed to Mr. Solomon Stein, a purple 3¢ stamp—with Thomas Jefferson's solemn profile peering out from under four heavy, wavy black lines—posing askew in the top right-hand corner of the envelope.

Also adorning the coffee table is a boxy Philco "Transitone" radio. Rectangular and made of brown plastic, it features a waffle semicircle insert of gold grille cloth. Looks like a turtle's shell, Seth notes, and beneath it, for feet, are two round knobs straddling the station numbers: 55 . . . 60 . . . 70 . . . 80 . . . 100 . . . 120 . . . 140 . . . 160.

On another small table squats a funky, squarish, large black rotary telephone whose face is pocked with little holes into which you insert your fingers to dial numbers. Its body is attached to the receiver by a six-foot-long, gnarly, twisted black coil. The phone number of the Stein residence is typed on a round white paper label on its nose: ULster 3-1801.

On the floor, adjacent to a red-and-black houndstooth armchair, a clunky Victrola phonograph languishes, its exhausted arm resting on a little metal platform, its single viper's fang protruding, poised to bite into the grooves of one of the 78 rpm vinyl records scattered nearby: *Tosca, Iolanthe, Guys and Dolls, Call Me Madam.*

A *Time* magazine with Bert Lahr on the cover—he's wearing a New York Giants baseball cap and mugging in front of a Wizard of Oz background—spreads itself out on the seat of the chair. On the arm is a book of matches with

WHITE OWL CIGARS printed on it, accompanied by a pack of cigarettes, three of them jutting out, with the black letters LUCKY STRIKE "IT'S TOASTED" inside a red target logo on the front.

Papa Sol smoked? And Grandma Elsie?

A dull thud from somewhere below. Then another. And a scraping noise.

Burglars?

Seth opens the door on the right and descends the twelve rickety wooden stairs leading to the basement. He hangs two quick lefts, heads to where he thinks the sound is emanating from. On his right, all along the wall, hangs a pantheon of ten neatly framed pictures of New York Giants greats: Mathewson, McGinnity, Marquard, Merkle, Stengel, Terry, Hubbell, Ott, Mize, Irvin.

At the end of the long, dimly lit main part of the basement hunches a man who seems to be doing some kind of repair work. The man is working with a tool. The man is toiling over a piece of furniture. Seth stops when he is about three feet from the man.

The man is Papa Sol.

Something is caught in Seth's throat, something that feels vaguely like a chicken bone. A tear wells up in the corner of his right eye and desiccates before it can descend the length of his cheek.

He takes a deep breath and a long look at this man, this younger, more robust version of Solomon Stein the Elder.

Papa Sol seems to be in his early twenties. But wait. It's 1951, so Seth does the math. Sol was born in 1928, so he must be . . . twenty-three.

This is the first time he has ever witnessed Solomon Stein doing his carpentry thing. Papa Sol always wanted his privacy when he worked. Said that as much as he loved

Seth and Elsie, he couldn't concentrate when he was being watched.

Sol is wearing a navy-and-red-checked flannel shirt, gray gabardine slacks, and a pair of battered old Red Wing work boots. What Seth notices most is that he is not wearing a beard. Never seen him clean-shaven, and he notices, too, that Papa Sol is quite the devilishly handsome young man. Despite that wicked magenta scar that runs down the side of his left cheek. It appears to be a keloid, possibly the result of an injury or an accident?

Funny, Papa Sol never mentioned it.

Sol's face presages the one Seth has known since he was little. The salient features are still prominent: the thick, rich head of jet-black hair, pepper not yet specked with salt; the penetrating, close-together brown eyes, intense and cheery; the charmingly Semitic nose, compliments of his father, Jacob, and his sturdy Russian-Jewish genes; the dark lips, curled up habitually in an incipient smile.

And, of course, the hands. The Michelangelo's *David* hands.

They are putting the finishing touches to the backrest of an oak chair, gouging out the wood surrounding the head of one of two men playing chess. As in a Flemish painting within a painting, the two chess players are themselves seated on chairs with the very same backrests as the one Sol is working on.

The exquisiteness of his grandfather's artistry enthralls Seth. The delicate way Sol manipulates his chisel, caressing the wood with slow, measured movements. Each wood shaving is paper-thin, and before it drops to the floor, Sol looks at it with a tinge of sadness, as if to bid it a fond adieu, to apologize for removing it from its original site. It is as if the chisel were Maestro Sol's baton, the wood his symphony orchestra.

Papa Sol is the eighth dwarf, Busy, whistling while he works. How Seth misses his impassioned, trilly whistling. Used to whistle all kinds of stuff to his grandson, from commercial jingles and popular songs to show tunes and opera arias. Now it is "The Flowers That Bloom in the Spring," from Gilbert and Sullivan's *The Mikado,* that soothes Seth's savage breast.

Seth is engulfed by a powerful urge to talk to his Papa Sol. His brain—protesting not only that Sol can't see or hear him, but also that he hasn't chronologically had a grandson yet—is peremptorily overruled by his heart.

"Papa Sol. It's me, your Setharoo."

Sol steps back to consider his handiwork. "Not bad for a young whippersnapper, I must admit. Nice work, Solomon Stein."

"It is so good to see you again. I miss you *so* much—"

"Still needs a bit of work around the chessboard, though. Maybe a little filing."

"And so does Grandma Elsie—"

"And the cheek of the player on the left needs to be smaller, and flatter maybe."

"Papa Sol, why did you disappear? *What the hell happened—*"

"Hmmm . . . gotta get up early tomorrow. Better pack it in."

"It's so strange seeing you like this, you as a young man. Strange but nice all the same. Papa Sol—"

"Sol honey? Time to come up now. It's nearly eight, and you don't wanna miss your Uncle Miltie!"

The voice of twenty-two-year-old Elsie Adler Stein, urgent and ululant, echoes down the basement stairs, interrupting the disconnected monologues of Solomon Stein and his grandson. It's time for Sol to come up to bed.

Sol sweeps up the mess, puts away his chisel, negotiates the twenty-eight stairs from basement to bedroom. Seth, invisible shadow, follows close behind, his brain abuzz with reflection.

How freaky to see Papa Sol again, as a young man. Sol at twenty-three! Sol without a beard! Sol doing his carpentry! He never let me watch him work, but he used to talk all the time about this passion of his. Used to tell me how a bad carpenter blames his tools. How he was the last in a long line of great Jewish carpenters that began with Jesus. One of my favorite poems he used to read to me was Lewis Carroll's "The Walrus and the Carpenter." And I remember the first lines of poetry he ever taught me, written by Anne Sexton, and how I memorized them and first became aware of the instinctive side of being a carpenter:

> *But suicides have a special language.*
> *Like carpenters they want to know* which tools.
> *They never ask* why build.

How lucky some people are to be able to do one thing brilliantly. Willie Mays and his baseball. Leo Kottke and his guitar. Papa Sol and his carpentry.

Solomon Stein is brusha-brusha-brushing his teeth with Ipana dental paste, having left Seth in his wake. Seth stands at the threshold of the bedroom, staring at both the squat little television and the lovely young woman in the bed, his grandmother-to-be.

Leaning back on two feather pillows, Elsie Stein positions herself in a supine pose reminiscent of Goya's *La Maja Vestida*. Unlike the painting's provocative damsel, Elsie is bedecked in thick pink flannel pj's dotted with big red hearts and is watching commercials.

> *Halo, everybody, Halo,*
> *Halo is the shampoo that glorifies your hair.*
> *So Halo, everybody, Halo!*

Seth is pleasantly stunned to see his future grand-mother as a young woman, with her customary smile instead of the recent frown. With skin that is smooth and taut, not rough and wrinkled. In perky jammies, in contrast to a matronly nightgown.

Of secondary importance, but no less fascinating, is the television, a twelve-inch-screen, antediluvian beaut of a Du-Mont. It is more like a piece of furniture, the tiny raft of a screen floating in an ocean of mahogany. Its odd hexagonal shape resembles a doghouse, with little wooden pedestals protruding from the bottom. Five funky buttons below the screen, in lieu of a remote—one on the left, four on the right, for on-off, volume, contrast, tuning. To the right of the screen are six funny-looking slits in the wood with cloth behind them, and below them, a small, round, glass-covered opening revealing two horizontal black bars on a lit orange background, to indicate that the TV is on, then a large wheel—the first, troglodytic TV invention?—that you turned around and around and around, painstakingly and clockwise, to get to the desultory dearth of individual channels: 2, 4, 5, 7, 9, 11, 13.

> *Use Ajax (bum bum),*
> *the foaming cleanser (bum-a-bum-a-bum bum bum),*

floats the dirt . . .
right down the drain (bum-a-bum-a-bum-a-bum).

"You almost done in there, sweets? Mr. Television'll be on in a minute or two!"
"Ahl me rah ing, mng dallig!"

Brylcreem, a little dab'll do ya . . .

"Okeydokey, Elsie m'love, here I come!"

Hey Mabel, Black Label!

Seth turns his eyes away from the Carling beer commercial to see Sol crawl into bed and give Elsie a loving look for the ages. Sol settles in, holds Elsie's hand, and they are ready to watch their favorite program, Tuesday night's *Texaco Star Theater*, starring their Uncle Miltie, the incomparable Milton Berle.

Six eyes are now trained on the teeny DuMont screen. A curtain rises, and four Texaco servicemen pop out, lined up side by side, marching in place, in lockstep, dressed in gas attendant suits, bow ties, and Texaco caps, each one holding a tool of his trade: wrench, nozzle, rag, hubcap.

Oh, we're the men of Texaco,
We work from Maine to Mexico,
There's nothing like this Texaco of ours . . .

"Sweetheart?" Sol says.
"Yes, my pudding face?"
"Listen, I'm going to the game tomorrow, as you know,

and it's a really, really big one, as you know, and I was thinking I have that extra ticket Nat gave me because he couldn't go, and I was thinking that maybe Simon could come with me?"

Our show tonight is powerful,
We'll wow you with an hour full
Of howls from a showerful of stars . . .

Simon?, Seth thinks. *My dad?* He must be . . . 1951 minus 1948 . . . three!

"Honey," Elsie responds with gravity. "You know how I feel about this. Simon's only three, fer chrissakes. You can't take him to a ball game, with all that screaming and carrying on and craziness. Not until he's older, at least. He's *three*! And that's final!"

We're the merry Texaco men,
Tonight we may be showmen,
Tomorrow we'll be servicing your cars!

"But, sweetie pie, this is *baseball*! And you're never too young to go to a baseball game. And Simon would have an absolute ball, and I've often seen kids at games who were even young—"

"No, no, no, no, and no!"

I wipe the pipe
I pump the gas
I rub the hub . . .

"Lovey-dovey, listen to me. I *do* know how young Simon is. But . . .

I touch the clutch
I mop the top
I poke the choke . . .

". . . we're talkin' baseball here. It isn't just any old game. It teaches a kid passion and resilience and humility and sacrifice, and you can never be too young to—"

I clear the gear
I block the knock
I jack the back . . .

"I know, I know," Elsie says, appreciating Sol's passion. Seth appreciates it, too.

Elsie sits up in bed, crosses her arms on her chest. *"I hear you, my dear, but . . . the queen has spoken!"*

Sol so wants to take Simon to the ball game, but he also loves Elsie too much to press on. He contorts his face into a moue, protrudes his pouty bottom lip so it covers his top one, furls his eyebrows, and emits a poorly faked, pathetic whimper.

All three present in the room crack up.

And now, the star of our show, Milton Berle!

"Good evening, ladies and germs . . ."

Shelving his disappointment, Papa Sol, in his suavest Paul Henreid move, lights up two Luckies in his mouth, places one between his parted lips and one between Elsie's. They take in long, deep lungfuls of smoke and, hissing softly, exhale them languorously between their teeth.

An intense look between the two future grandparents expresses an ineffable nuance of love that a dictionary could not provide.

Standing at the threshold, a kvelling Seth shares the joy.

Uncle Miltie is doing his black-and-white thing on-screen. He is dressed in drag: dark lipstick, ridiculous Carmen Miranda–style fruit hat, frilly dress, six gaudy necklaces, high heels.

Seth has never seen anything like it before. Whacked-out, slapstick, manic, frenetic, over-the-top stuff. But *fun-ny*. A muffled, embarrassed laugh escapes from his mouth.

"Excuse me, sir. Yes, you, in the front row. Is that your wife sitting next to you?"

"Why, yes."

"Well, now I know why married men live longer than single men. Or maybe it just *seems* longer." [*Rimshot. Audience screams with delight.*]

Berle does one of his patented double takes, mugs at the camera, presses his lips against the camera lens and kisses it. He mugs again, trips and picks himself up, gawkily and unladylike. The audience howls.

Seth can't suppress a guffaw. Since no one can hear him, he sneaks in another, even louder one. Sol and Elsie laugh uncontrollably.

"Y'know, folks, I'm only kiddin', only kiddin'. Actually, marriage is a great institution, but who wants to live in an institution?" [*Rimshot. Hysterical laughter.*]

"My uncle believes that marriage and a career don't mix, so when he got married he stopped working!" [*Rimshot. Earsplitting chortles.*]

"I told my wife that a husband is like a fine wine—he gets better with age. The next day she locked me in the cellar." [*Rimshot. Absolute bedlam.*]

Uncle Miltie trots offstage.

Sol and Elsie take another drag on their Luckies. Seth chuckles unabashedly.

You can trust your car to the man who wears the star,
The big, bright Texaco star . . .

Berle returns onstage, this time dressed as a caveman wearing nothing but a stupid leopard-skin outfit, black socks, and wingtip shoes. He rat-a-tats a furious volley of seven consecutive prehistoric one-liners.

Seth is beside himself with hysteria, and so are Sol and Elsie. This continues for the next fifty minutes *solid.* Except during brief appearances by singer Yma Sumac and actor John Carroll, and a few more Texaco commercials, the bedroom is filled with wall-to-wall laughter, as Miltie executes pratfalls, one-liners, double takes, triple takes, and assorted shtick, pursing his Señor Wences "Johnny" lips, flashing his phony buck-toothed smiles. The three bedroom spectators guffaw nearly nonstop. By the time Mr. Television sings his trademark tearjerker "Near You" at the show's conclusion, their six sides hurt so much, they can laugh no more.

Near you. Exactly how Seth feels at this moment toward Papa Sol and Grandma Elsie. Just seeing Sol again. Seeing Sol and Elsie together like this. All that laughter, all that love.

"Hey, Else, I'm beat," Sol says, sighing.

"Me, too, sweetie pie."

"I love you so much."

"Love you, too."

Elsie turns off the TV, and by the time she gets back into bed, Sol is snoring. She turns off her night table lamp and plants a smooch on Sol's forehead.

Seth is feeling awkward, standing there alone like an idiot. He wheels around, notices a night-light coming from a smaller bedroom across the hall. Peeking in, he spies a toddler fast asleep in a small bed, tucked under a multicolored Captain Marvel and Shazam blanket. He approaches the bed and, on closer inspection, sees that the toddler bears an eerie resemblance to Seth himself, and to Sammy.

The toddler is Simon Stein, his father.

Twenty-two years before he was even born, Seth is checking in on his slumbering three-year-old dad. He fights the urge to wake the boy up and hug him tight and say how he loves him and he's so very sorry how things turned out and, oh, how he would've liked to have known him.

In the pitch black, Seth Stein descends the sixteen stairs to the first floor, takes a seat on one of the three kitchen chairs.

Seth rubs his eyes. Feels a bit off, groggy really. Maybe it's just being here and all the walking and all the strangeness and all the emotion and seeing Papa Sol, and then Papa Sol with Grandma Elsie, and now checking in on his toddler father. Feels almost like being in the middle of one of those dreamy, soft dissolves, the kind you see in the movies . . .

ⓒ

At the other end of the dissolve, Seth Stein sits on a stiff, narrow green wooden seat. He rubs his eyes again, begins to regain his focus. All around him is still hazy but becoming clearer by the second. Now he can see much better. There.

Ohmygodohmygodohmygodohmygodohmygodohmygodohmygod.

Picture Sylvester the Cat in love. Picture that cartoon heart of his beating four feet out of his chest, that swollen, pulsating, vermilion heart, umbilically connected to his body and miraculously suspended in midair, ba-booming like a kettle drum for the newfound object of his feline affection. Such is the manic fibrillation of Seth's coronary muscle.

His head, to the contrary, is executing a very steady, very controlled, very slow, very wide shot, all in one take, panning from left to right and covering the entire 180 degrees of which his neck is capable. At each juncture of the pan, his brain registers data he is witnessing for the first time but that he knows intimately nonetheless, gleaned from a wondrous fairy tale Papa Sol had recited to him, in exquisite detail and with frightful frequency, over the years.

There's the left-field bull pen just below . . . the 447-foot sign in left-center . . . the nook in dead center, an unthinkable 485 feet away from home plate, and the two bleacher sections and the clubhouse building in between and the Chesterfield sign, yes, with the words ALWAYS BUY CHESTERFIELD and, above them, A HIT! inside a smoke ring coming from the end of a cigarette and the square Longines clock with the flagpole above . . . the 440-foot sign in right-center . . . the two-tiered grandstands in right . . . the pack of Chesterfields and the scoreboard and the 258-foot sign at the right-field line . . . all that space in foul territory . . . the huge horseshoe-shaped stands behind home plate . . . the pack of Chesterfields and the scoreboard and the 279-foot sign at the left-field line . . . the two-tiered grandstands in left . . .

Here sits Seth, on a green wooden seat in the upper deck of the left-field grandstands, above the visiting bull pen in the Mecca of New York Giants baseball fans and

Papa Sol's beloved rooting home field. The old bathtub, the odd-shaped horseshoe, the rickety, asymmetrical, funky, weirdly constructed object of Jints fans' adoration. Between Coogan's Bluff and the Harlem River, at 155th Street and Eighth Avenue, in the Bronx, New York. Where the fans sit far away from the action, the bull pens are in play, foul territory is too voluminous, the foul lines are too short, and center field too deep. "The Parthenon it ain't," Papa Sol used to say.

The Polo Grounds!

So far, this panorama has accounted for 179 degrees of the pan. At degree number 180, the head stops. The final frame of the shot, now an extreme close-up, captures the spectator sitting next to Seth in the stands, in the seat to his immediate right.

It is Papa Sol.

Seth's eyes are glued to twenty-three-year-old Solomon Stein, whose eyes are glued to the playing field.

"I love you, Papa Sol," he blurts, touching his grandfather on the shoulder, squeezing it, hoping that this time, somehow, Sol might hear and see and feel him.

Nada.

Seth is letting it sink in, every morsel of it, including, now, his Papa Sol by his side. On Sol's lap is today's unopened paper, a *New York Herald Tribune*. The date underneath the masthead catches Seth's eye: October 3, 1951.

October 3, 1951. A date drilled into him by fanatical New York Giants baseball fan Solomon Stein. Seth knows the date by heart, like the back of his hand. Knows it like he knows October 19, 1973, the day he was born. Like he knows June 10, 2003, the day he first laid eyes on his darling Kate. Like he knows July 4, 1776, and December 7, 1941, and November 22, 1963, and September 11, 2001, and all those other crucial dates embedded in the library stacks of his brain.

October 3, 1951. One of the immutable, indelible days in American history. A day of great moment, the day of the Miracle of Coogan's Bluff, of the Shot Heard 'Round the World, of the Giants' miracle comeback and last-ditch victory over the Dodgers, of the Ultimate Game in the ultimate game of the '51 pennant playoffs, of the great Russ Hodges, announcing on the radio, hoarsely propelling, in a four-part, four-gun salute to triumph and destiny, the unforgettable "The Giants Win the Pennant!" into the all-time annals of our National Pastime and our Historical Consciousness.

Now that Seth thinks of it, he has never personally witnessed a real, live historical event, not until now. And this one's a doozy. He's only heard about this game, boy, has he heard about it.

And now he's here.

How many times had Papa Sol, his own personal baseball mentor, recounted to him this made-for-Hollywood movie, in CinemaScope and Technicolor? Told him about how significant this game was, about the bitter Giants-Dodgers rivalry, about Leo the Lip leaving the hated Dodgers in '48 to replace the Giants' beloved skip Mel Ott, about the nail-biting, gut-wrenching '51 pennant race between these two teams from the same city, who despised each other, about Leo bringing Willie Mays up from Minny and sticking with the green rookie despite his 1-for-27 start and switching Irvin and Lockman in left field and first base and switching Thomson from center to third when Willie joined the club, about the Giants being behind the Dodgers by a laughable thirteen and a half games on August 11 with a mere forty-four to play and then winning sixteen in a row and thirty-seven of their final forty-four and catching the Dodgers with one to play and then, to force a playoff, the Dodgers themselves had to come from behind 6–1 against the Phillies on the last day of the season (Robby's homer off Robin Roberts winning it in the fourteenth), about Bobby Thomson homering off Ralph Branca to win the first play-off game, 3–1, and the Jints getting drubbed in the second, 10–0, and the glorious, magnificent rubber game . . .

And then there's all the trivia Papa Sol had spoon-fed to him concerning the ninth inning of the final game: Hartung pinch-running for Mueller, Mays being on deck when Bobby hit the big one, Lou Jorda umping behind the plate . . .

Seth glances at the big scoreboard to his right:

BKLYN 1000000
N.Y. 000000

Bottom of the seventh. Seth knows all the numbers by heart and fills in the final two and a half innings in his mind's eye:

BKLYN 100000030
N.Y. 000000104

No suspense for him, no emotional buildup. No matter, either, because he is *here*.

Seth Stein sits pensively in his little green wooden seat, next to his Papa Sol, on this particular October afternoon, and it is just sinking in. Here he is, watching not a baseball game, but a *classic*. He is watching it not as a spectator, but as a historian. For this is History, pure and simple. He knows it, knows it in his bones, in his gut. Knows how fortunate he is to be here, seeing the greatest, most important game in the history of American, no, of international sports, of all time, and to be not just seeing it, but to be seeing it in retrospect, in perspective, and in progress, all at once.

He smiles as he thinks of the old sports apothegm "Hindsight is twenty-twenty." Because he knows that of all the people in this stadium today, he alone can see clearly into the past, and indeed, in this bottom of the seventh inning, into the future. Because he knows that he is the only human being here, including the 34,320 paid spectators, who has the ability to predict the outcome of this game. Because he knows that through all the ebbs and flows, the highs and lows, the hope and despair, the rallying and falling behind, the silences and roars, the suspended breathing and exhalations of relief, the cheering and jeering, he is the only one here today capable of seeing it all as History.

It's almost enough to make you feel giddy.

The fans are finishing their seventh-inning stretches, hunkering back down to the deadly serious business of rooting, and here come the Dodgers spilling onto the field. They leap out of the visitors' dugout, all but their tiring fireballer, Don Newcombe, who trudges. They are facing Seth, all nine of them, exposing to him the fronts of their uniforms with the word DODGERS emblazoned on their chests, blue script letters on a gray background, letters only, before they started putting the numbers in red just below. But Seth doesn't need crib notes or a program: He knows all the numbers by heart. There's Billy Cox 3 and Pee Wee Reese 1 and Jackie Robinson 42 and Gil Hodges 14, around the horn in the infield. And in the outfield, there's Andy Pafko 22 (he'll become 48 next year, but no matter) and Duke Snider 4 and Carl Furillo 6, left to right.

And here comes the battery, Newk 36 and Roy Campanella 39, nope, that's right, Campy's hurt today, so it's Rube Walker 10.

Seth is struck by the whiteness of the players, noting that there are only two African Americans on the Dodgers' starting nine. *Two.* Newcombe and Robinson, that's it. Well, Campy usually catches, but when Newk's not on the mound, it'd still be two. Matter of fact, now that he thinks of it, the Giants also have only two black starters, Mays and Irvin. How long it took baseball to become an equal opportunity employer. But how long it took *all of society* to get with the program. After all, it's only 1951, and America isn't color-blind and has yet to see the likes of Chuck Berry and Rosa Parks and Althea Gibson and Malcolm X and MLK.

Hodges is tossing grounders to his infielders, and in the outfield they're playing catch, and Big Newk is, almost against his will, taking his eight warm-up pitches.

Seth pans around the ballpark again and drinks it all in, a bee sucking pollen from a jasmine tree. He can feel the zeitgeist: the spirit, the vibration, the nervousness not just of a crowd of people, but of an entire era. All the battle-weary, Commie-fearing, suspicious uptightness of postwar America, of Korean War America, of an America consumed by the rantings of Joe McCarthy the madman and a president in disfavor and the Rosenbergs sentenced to die for espionage and the Russian nuclear test on September 24, a mere nine days ago. By osmosis and instinct, he can feel the collective weltschmerz of it all, the paranoia and the fear.

He can feel all this, feel it in the marrow of his historian's bones. Can feel an America searching for heroes in these dire times. They are not finding one in their president, Harry S., the simple man from the Show-Me State who's an honest, direct, no bullshit kinda guy, the hero and savior of the Big War for dropping the Big One. But now Truman's in disfavor, what with firing poor old MacArthur, the seventy-one-year-old five-star general, and backing down from McCarthy and now the calls for impeachment and all. And so these fans, every one of them, are looking for someone else to uplift them and give them a reason to cheer, and it sure won't be Florence Chadwick, who just swam the English Channel to France in an incredible sixteen hours twenty-two minutes, because she's a woman, don't you know, and it's a little too early for that, and Seth alone knows who, today, that hero will be. And he is feeling it all now and tasting History happening and savoring it and smelling it and seeing it unfold before his very eyes and knowing that being here is, well, a whole different ball game.

"C'mon, you Jints! Let's get somethin' started!" Solomon Stein shouts.

Seth is startled out of his rumination by Papa Sol's stentorian entreaty. He is happy once again to see his grandfather so near, and so passionate about the game and the team they both love so.

Under his breath, Sol adds, "I'll never give up on you guys!"

This last sentence hits a nerve in Seth. Like you never gave up on us, on me and Grandma Elfie and Sammy and Kate?

Sol hunkers down as Monte Irvin, the former Negro League star and future Hall of Famer, steps up to the plate. Seth is watching his grandfather settle back into his rooting, passionate, resolute, intense. Seth always admired the passion, but, and this is not a big thing, he is a tad concerned as he watches. There is an edge to this passion of Papa Sol's that Seth is seeing for the first time, that he is finding mildly disturbing, an inward-directed, smoldering, intense something, gathering there in Sol's bosom, seething inside and perhaps needing an outlet as he sits there in his little wooden seat, sits and bides his time and watches big Monte dry his sweaty hands with a rosin bag.

The Giants fans are restless, all but the two Steins in attendance, Solomon sitting there in his tranquil fury and Seth knowing full well that Irvin's about to slap a double to left past Pafko and the Giants will tie it up, along with everything else that will transpire today.

Irvin slaps a double to left past Pafko.

"Dirty nigger!" is the venom a Dodger fan spews at the Giants left fielder from a seat somewhere in the next section over. Seated next to him is a young, droopy-shouldered black man, a Giants fan who dares not object to the racist taunt.

Seth cringes at the epithet. Not at the virulence of the venom itself, but at the fact that in over a half century, America has made progress in this area, yes, but not nearly enough.

Irvin takes his lead off second and the lefty first sacker Carroll Walter "Whitey" Lockman strides up to the batter's box and Solomon Stein sits there, brewing.

Lockman is up there now, staring Big Newk down, taking big, full counterfeit practice swings but up there for one reason only, to bunt and move Irvin over to third, ninety feet away from tying this thing up.

"C'mon, Whitey, you c'n do it," a Giants fan screams, just to Seth's left.

"This big ol' country boy from Podunk, N.C., he's got shit for brains," a Dodgers fan within earshot retorts. "An' on toppa that, he don't know shit from Shinola."

"Oh yeah?" the Jints fan ripostes. "He knows Shinola all right, it's *you* who don't know shit!"

"I know shit when I see it, buddy," the Bums backer—no doubt a disgruntled loser years ago in a *Happy Felton's Knothole Gang* competition—shoots back, making eye contact, "and I'm starin' at it right now!"

Seth takes in the maturity of the exchange, as well as the sweet irony of Whitey sacrificing himself for the good of a black man.

He takes a deep breath and inhales the mephitic stench of 15,000 cigarettes burning like the Queen Mary's smoke-stacks and the acrid odor of stale beer being swilled and spilled by another 15,000 attendees and the pungent aroma of mustard slathered on dogs and the saccharine scent of sticky Cracker Jacks and the musky bouquet of My Sin and Chanel No. 5 reeking from the veiled visages of ladies in the crowd.

His head does a few more camera moves, this time a se-ries of quick cuts from one grandstand section to the next. This place is a mess, a living, breathing, slovenly organism, up here in the nosebleed grandstands, and the aisles are bulging with paper cups of stale beer and cigarette butts and programs and peanut shells and crumpled cigarette packs—Old Golds, Luckies, Camels, Chesterfields, Pall Malls, Philip Morrises.

Irvin extends his lead off second and Newk comes to the stretch and Lockman squares around to bunt and the fans are all fidgety and Seth is watching the action with his historian's eyes but also observing the Polo Grounds, this gorgeous old bathtub of a stadium, which he knows in twelve and a half years—on April 10, 1964, to be exact—will be reduced to a pile of rubble and transformed into an apartment complex, The Polo Grounds Towers, with

Willie Mays Field, an asphalt playground with six basket-ball backboards, sitting right there, smack-dab in the middle of center field.

Whitey lays down a honey and catcher Walker tries to nail Irvin sliding into third instead of pegging to first for the sure out and the black man is in there safely and Whitey, too. First and third and now Bobby Thomson coming up to try to knock in the tying run.

As Bobby swings a couple of bats and ambles up to the dish, Seth is struck by the numbing drabness surrounding him. Ladies are wearing the same gray and brown dresses, black and brown veiled hats, an occasional auburn fox stole. Men are decked out in their fedoras, lots of them, all gray and tan and black, relieved only by an occasional sailor under a white sailor hat. And everybody, it seems, is dressed in solid colors: blacks, browns, and grays, sweaters, jackets, and ties, all melding into one another, unbroken by a houndstooth or a herringbone or a paisley or a stripe or a family crest. The pale redundancy of the colors in the crowd contrasts sharply with the action on the field: the brilliant emerald of the outfield and the rich umber humus of the infield and the dazzling, whirling uniforms on the battle-field.

Fittingly, the day is gray, sixty-degree gray, with the distinct threat of rain hovering like a shroud. The skies are dark, the stadium is dark, the colors in the stands are drab. There is a rawness to the day, and it isn't just the weather. It is the rawness of emotion, a frisson permeating the atmosphere, the nervous hammering of precisely 34,320 hearts worn on precisely 34,320 sleeves. It is raw out here, and the red and yellow and orange tongues of flame are darting inside every last one of these spectators, the inner fires of hatred and hope. They are all out for blood, one way or another, and it is the blood loyalty of these fans that gives a vitality to the proceedings, the Hatfields-and-McCoys blood loyalty passed on from one generation to the next, the helix of hope and hatred. Papa Sol used to tell Seth how Dodgers fans even hated Halloween, because of the orange-and-black colors of the Giants.

Seth muses about how the enmity of this rivalry is symptomatic of a thirst, in the America of the early fifties, for polarity. Back then—or right now, as the case may be— the entire complex network of matter in the cosmos, the totality of life and its endless nuances, had in many and profound ways been simplified, reduced, boiled down to the number *two*. An infinity of binarities. Always two rivals, two combatants, two sides. Us vs. Them. Yanks vs. Commies. White hat (Tex Ritter) vs. black hat (bad guy). Cowboys vs. Indians. Ipana vs. Colgate. Tide vs. Fab. Kellogg's vs. Post. Ethel Merman vs. Mary Martin. Perry Como vs. Eddie Fisher. Jints vs. Bums. And of the two, only one can be left standing. An America that could make Darwin sit up in his grave and beam with pride.

"Ladies and gentlemen, the official paid attendance for today's ball game is 34,320," the PA announcer divulges. A statistic baseball fanatic Seth Stein has known for nearly three decades.

Thomson lofts a towering fly to center, driving Snider back, far enough to score Irvin from third. Giants fans exhale. Dodgers fans groan. It is 1–1.

A parched throat and a killer thirst jolt Seth out of his reverie. He waves to the beer vendor, who fortuitously is passing by. He waves again, calls out.

"Yeah, one beer right here!" Seth says.

"Hey, getcha beer heah. Getcha cold beer he-ah . . ."

"One beer, please—"

"Hey, getcha cold Pabst Blue Ribbon right he-ah . . ."

"I'll have a Pabst—"

"Getcha ice-cold brew right heeeeee-ahhhh . . ."

Crap. Forgot the guy can't hear me.

Newk wriggles out of the inning, and it is the Giants who take the field now for the top of the eighth. Here they come, shooting stars onto the field, a bonfire of bodies ignited by the recent rally. Mo is on their side, largely responsible for the newfound hop in their collective step.

Seth knows better.

Here they come toward him, and again Seth prognosticates numbers: Bobby Thomson 23 and Alvin Dark 19 and Eddie Stanky 12 and Whitey Lockman 25, then Monte Irvin 20 and Willie Mays 24 and Don Mueller 22, then the battery, Sal Maglie 35 and Wes Westrum 9.

Wes Westrum! How Papa Sol loved this stocky, dependable catcher. Seth recites his catechism to himself. Wesley Noreen Westrum. Born November 28, 1922, in Clearbrook, Minnesota. Solid as a rock behind the plate. Called one helluva game. Good glove: had .999 fielding percentage in 1950. No hit: had career BA of .217. Funniest quote Sol ever taught him came from Wes's mouth and said volumes about the receiver's artful command of the English language. When he was managing the woeful Mets in the midsixties and they pulled out a long, extra-inning game, he was later grilled by reporters. "So, Wes, what are your thoughts about the game?" one journalist asked. Wes scratched his head, reflected for a moment, and replied, "Well, it was a real cliff dweller."

The top of the eighth is a bane for Giants fans, a boon for Dodgers rooters. Papa Sol sits, stoic and seething. Seth spectates with a calm neutrality, knowing the Dodgers will soon score three times and lead 4–1, only to be ultimately caught and passed. But all around them is bedlam.

Pee Wee singles, motors into third on the Dook's single to right. The cobra, Sal the Barber, wild-pitches Robby, his personal mongoose, and Reese scores, with Snider reaching second safely. Now the roof falls in. Robinson is intentionally walked, Thomson butchers a drive by Pafko, then another one by Cox. It is 4–1 before you know it, and half of the Polo Grounds, filled with joy, is shrieking long and loud in a collective orgasm, while the other half, filled with despair, is cursing the day they were born.

At inning's end, a disconsolate Maglie traipses from mound to dugout, Sol gives him an empathetic look from afar, and Seth is recalling the bedtime story "The Saga of Sad-Sack Sal" that Papa Sol recounted to him once when he was five. About how poor Sal knocked around for a while in Mexico and finally made it to the bigs full time at the tender age of thirty-three. And about how he just shrugged it off, like a catcher's bad sign, and proceeded to compile the greatest won-lost record for his first full three years—a jaw-dropping 59–18, for a percentage of .766—of any pitcher ever. By a whopping .95 points. Better than Cy Young and Christy Mathewson and Grover Cleveland Alexander and Walter Johnson and Bob Gibson and Nolan Ryan and *anyone!*

"C'mon, you guys, I know you c'n do it!" Sol implores his Giants, who have just finished trudging off the field. He is still hopeful, but a solemn glare is all his eyes can muster.

"Hey, bub, why don't you just shadaaaaaaap, huh?" a sophisticated fan yells affectionately from above. To no avail: Sol is there but not there, so totally wrapped up in this, so inside himself, that he is oblivious to his friendly neighbor's imprecations.

A wet towel suffocates the hopes of Sol and about eighteen thousand other Giants fans: In their half of the eighth, pinch hitters Rigney and Thompson strike out and tap meekly back to the mound, respectively, and the usually pesky Stanky fans for the third out.

As the dejected Jints take the field for the top of the ninth, Seth Stein ruminates. He is thinking about baseball as History. How this extraordinary game is not just a game, but—perhaps more than political machinations or global events or wars or changes in governments—a metaphor that represents, in some profound way, History itself. How its metaphorical criteria include the passing down of passions and information to future generations, the learning of life lessons, the learning from past experience, the learning from winning and losing, the overcoming of obstacles, the coping with ebb and with flow, the performing of actions under pressure and a microscope, the creation of a crucible in which ordinary events and people can be transformed, momentarily, into heroic entities.

Baseball has always been and always will be, he is thinking, a sign of the times, a continuum. Thanks to its fans, players from the past—some long gone—live in the present and well into the future. Their personae, their statistics, their records, the numbers on their backs, even their most insignificant and stupefyingly idiotic idiosyncrasies live on compellingly, entering the brains and hearts of countless millions of passionate strangers, generation after generation, to be buried with their bones or burned with their ashes.

Then there are the eternal routines and rituals that remain changeless, from 1869 to 1951 to 2033 and onward. The faithful maintenance of dizzying stats and the parochial lingo known to every true fan and the mindless infield chatter like no language known to humankind and the pregame fungo and the warm-up pitches and the practice catches in the outfield and the on-deck circles and the dugout ribbing and the dumb practical jokes and the rhubarbs and the ground rules and the spitting of tobacco juice and sunflower seeds and phlegm. Reminds Seth of the old Bill Veeck quote: "Baseball is the only thing besides the paper clip that hasn't changed."

And this pennant race of 1951, and this final, climactic playoff game that Seth feels privileged to be witnessing, what more glowing example could a person find of metaphor, of History?

Seth is aware of some sort of movement, subtle at first, but there it is. A vague rumbling, a distinct but nuanced flow of bodies around him, getting up, grabbing coats, moving out. For the first time in the game, fans are beginning to drift toward the exits. It is the top of the ninth, New York is down by three, and apparently some not-so-die-hard Giants fans have given up hope. Seth assumes they are Giants fans, since even the least committed of Dodgers fans would never, *ever* leave the stadium, with their team leading 4–1, until they had savored the final out, the final nail in the proverbial coffin.

The top of the ninth passes briskly and without fanfare, a breeze of an inning for Larry Jansen, one of the Giants' stalwart starters all year, who had come in to relieve a fatigued and battered Sal the Barber.

Now it is the fateful bottom of the ninth, the bottom of the ninth Seth knows by heart, the bottom of the ninth that will electrify the civilized world.

Here comes Alvin Dark sauntering up to the plate, the all-American pretty-boy football hero from LSU who years later will be accused of being a racist, coming up to the plate with, ironically, his trademark black bat in tow. And for the first time since Seth found himself here at the game,

Papa Sol gets up. Until now, he hasn't stood up or stretched or left to get a hot dog or a pack of Luckies or gotten up to pee. Has just sat there, riveted to the painted green wooden slats of his seat.

Sol not only gets up, but he sidesteps out to the aisle, walks up steps, appears to be leaving. Seth follows close behind, puzzled. Maybe he needs to take a leak?

Sol moves past the stench of the public restrooms, descends the ramp, and now is on the lower grandstand level. Could he be leaving, with all the rest of the Giants fans who've surrendered and given in to defeat and despair? Doesn't sound like Papa Sol.

Sol is walking down the steps now, on the lower level of seats, closer to the field, closer to the left-field wall. Maybe now that people are beginning to file out, there'll be a seat closer to the action. Maybe Sol just wants to get away from that moron who was screaming at him.

There, there's an empty one over there, in fact three empty seats in a row, and it's three rows up from the wall and right off the aisle and now Dark is standing at the plate in his familiar crouch, cocking his wrists so that black bat of his is parallel to the ground, and Sol plops down in his new seat and so does invisible Seth.

The Giants fans in the crowd come to life, slowly at first, then with a little more hope in their voices, as Dark bleeds a single to right that nicks Hodges's glove and Mueller follows suit with another bleeder to nearly the identical spot. Must be Kismet or something, the crowd must be thinking. Those never-say-die Giants are at it again.

Irvin steps up to the plate, the always dependable Monte, to continue the last-ditch rally. The Giants' candle is still flickering, but barely.

As Monte does his rosin bag thing, Seth happens to

look to his left and slightly behind him, looks at the huge column of steel that supports the upper deck, registers in his encyclopedic brain the two white numbers painted on the front of the column and just above the level of his head. Thirty-five. This is Section 35.

Jeez Louise.

And the overanxious Irvin fouls out meekly to Hodges and the Giants fans go limp and the Dodgers fans are really into it now, it's their turn to scream and the momentum has changed once again. The Giants are down to their final two outs and it's almost curtains and now it's all up to Whitey Lockman and then Bobby Thomson on deck and Seth knows he's sitting in Section 35 and is even closer to History.

Man alive.

And Whitey flails at a high outside pitch and strokes a scorcher over third past Cox and just inside the foul line and into the corner and the Giants fans are going nuts and the Dodgers fans are squirming and Pafko chases it down and Dark scores and Lockman breezes into second and Mueller tears his ankle to shreds stumbling into third on his non-slide and they cart him off on a stretcher and Hartung runs for him and Big Newk is toast and Dressen brings in number 13, big Ralph Branca, 'cause Oisk is bouncing the curve in the pen and here comes the Flying Scot Robert Brown Thomson to the plate with the score 4–2 and the tying runs in scoring position and himself the winning run and Seth knows exactly what's gonna happen and *ohmydeargod* here I am, sitting next to Papa Sol, sitting right here in Section 35.

And Bobby takes a fastball right down the pipe and shit he shoulda swung at that one, the Giants fans are thinking, and he'll never get another good one 'cause Branca'll come back with Uncle Charlie and now Ralph winds up and delivers and crap it's another goddam fastball, the Dodgers fans are screaming silently, and why didn't the dumb sonuvabitch go with the curve? and the fastball's up and in and not a pitch to hit at all but Bobby catches it just right and tomahawks it, I mean he coldcocks it good, with plenty of topspin and mustard, and *there's a long drive . . . it's gonna be . . . I believe . . .*

And this is History and Seth is here seeing it and smelling it and tasting it and he glances at the Longines clock in center and yup sure enough it says 3:58 just like Papa Sol told him and the Polo Grounds simultaneously erupts with ecstasy and sags with disgust as the ball Bobby hits is tied to a rope but begins to spin downward and will it clear the fence? and now it is sailing right over Andy Pafko's limp body, Pafko standing there helpless in a heap of strewn paper and beer cups and cigarette butts and ticket stubs, and somehow it sails miraculously under the upper deck that is hanging defiantly fifteen feet in front of the left-field wall and dips crazily below the overhang and the ball just clears the 16.81-foot green concrete wall, clears it just barely and disappears somewhere into the lower left-field stands and half the crowd goes berserk.

Seth has heard the story a thousand times maybe, straight from the lips of his Papa Sol, but this is different. He is here, and he is watching *The Giants Win The Pennant!* But something *else* is different, and here it comes.

And the ball is coming toward Seth and Papa Sol and the fans all around them are cheering and whooping it up and hugging one another or else cursing and screaming *sonuvabitch!* and ripping up their programs and no one seems to know exactly where the ball has gone and who cares? but Seth who already knew what would happen is following the precise flight of the ball for History's sake and here it comes and it smashes into the steel column, smashes right into it, not on the flat front part but on its edge, obliquely, like a pointer when you're playing stoop-ball with a Spaldeen and it has lots of topspin so it bounces down and to the left and here it comes on a fly right toward Papa Sol's back and Papa Sol sort of senses where it is behind him and the ball is still spinning down, down . . .

Seth is speechless as, in one seamless split second of an instant, no, a split millisecond of an instant, the ball is snared, crisply and unnoticed, by the mighty left hand of Papa Sol, this carpenter's hand of his that clamps down on the ball clean and sure and pure, plucking it out of the air nearly invisibly, like a chameleon nabbing a beetle from a distant leaf with its silent, stealthy, sticky tongue before the poor unsuspecting bug knows what hit him.

It all happens so quickly, like a single beat of a hummingbird's wing, that no one in the ballpark notices it, no one except for Seth, that is. To him, it is a catch of miraculous proportions even greater than Willie's over-the-shoulder, back-to-the-plate catch off Vic Wertz in the '54 Series, or Ron Swoboda's diving, sprawling, one-handed grab off Brooks Robinson in the '69 Series, because it is executed backhanded, and blind, with Sol's back to the ball and with forty or so screaming, jumping, distracting, maniac fans surrounding him, to boot.

No one in the Polo Grounds has the slightest inkling of where the ball has landed, no one but the two Steins in the middle of all the bedlam, and fans are jumping under seats and scrambling around clueless, like rats in a maze, in a crazed and abortive search for a baseball that is not there.

And there stands Sol, cool as a chickpea and not moving a muscle, stands there stock-still so the enemy won't notice him, just like Lieutenant Dunbar in *Stalag 17* standing motionless in the water tank with his legs freezing like hell, and the ball is safely hidden in the impressive palm of Papa Sol's left hand and his right hand, clasping the top of his left one, presses the ball firmly against his chest and he is filled with joy at the Giants' victory but can't get too excited and risk dropping the ball or tipping someone off as to its precise whereabouts.

Seth stands there beside a happy Papa Sol, watching him, still speechless. It all happens so fast, before you can say Jack Robinson, and now Seth is having a flashback (*can I have a flashback if I'm already in one?*).

It is the year 2000, he is twenty-seven, and he has just finished reading the prologue to Don DeLillo's amazing novel *Underworld.* He is so excited to be reading about the Bobby Thomson pennant game, and he is telling Papa Sol all about Cotter Martin, the black kid in the novel who sneaks into the Polo Grounds and ends up fighting Bill Waterson for the famous ball and wrestling it away from Bill and keeping it—the actual Bobby Thomson ball! And after telling Papa Sol all this, he remembers to this day hearing his grandfather's strange laugh and how a surprisingly petulant Papa Sol shot back something to the effect that, "Well, it's fiction, what do you expect, and those goddam novelists can make up whatever flights of pure fantasy they damn well please!"

And Seth realizes that this is not a novel now, this is the real deal. And it is not the fictional character Cotter Martin who ended up with Bobby Thomson's historic blast, or anyone else on the planet for that matter.

It is Solomon Stein.

Seth is feeling exhausted, and a little light-headed. Could it be all this excitement? He rubs his eyes . . .

⚾

. . . and he is standing behind Papa Sol in the basement of 1270 Forty-ninth Street in Brooklyn, New York.

It is October 11, 1951, eight days after the big game. Seth knows that, because a copy of a local paper sitting right there on Papa Sol's workbench says so. Sol has cut two articles out of the sports section.

Sol walks to the basement cabinet, opens the bottom drawer, pulls out his personal baseball scrapbook, which is tucked way in the back, under a pile of rags. Before Sol closes the drawer, Seth notices a baseball way in the back, too, a baseball with a nasty one-inch-long blackish scuff mark, a ball that looks very much like the one Papa Sol left for him in that handcrafted wooden box.

Sol picks up the two articles and, one by one, pastes them with great care in the scrapbook. He scrutinizes them both as Seth watches him from behind.

The headline of the first article is YANKS NIP JINTS 4–3 IN GAME 6 DESPITE NINTH-INNING RALLY, TAKE SERIES, 4–2.

And the second: HUNDREDS OF FANS CLAIM TO OWN BOBBY THOMSON HOME-RUN BALL.

Solomon Stein has a funny look on his face as he rereads the second newspaper clipping. Funny as in odd.

Seth skims the same article, from just behind his grandfather. Something about hundreds of letters pouring in to newspaper editors and radio stations, written by earnest baseball fans who swear that they were at the game, sitting right there in Section 35, and that they, *and nobody else,* owned the famous Bobby Thomson clout. Caught it on the fly or dug it out from under the seats or grabbed it off of somebody else or whatever.

Seth thinks how bizarre and how can people lie like

that? And then he remembers a quote he learned way back in one of his undergrad World History courses, attributed to David and Leigh Eddings:

The notion that any one person can describe "what really happened" is an absurdity. If ten—or a hundred—people witness an event, there will be ten—or a hundred—different versions of what took place.

And he thinks how true the quote is, except in this particular case, if Sol described "what really happened" that afternoon in the Polo Grounds, it would *not* be an absurdity, he would in fact be telling the truth, the only correct version of what took place.

Seth is still pondering and doesn't notice Sol getting up and going back to the same bottom cabinet drawer and now he does notice and Papa Sol reaches in the back of the drawer and removes what appears to be a .38-caliber Smith & Wesson revolver and checks to see if there are cartridges in the cylinder.

Papa Sol owned a handgun?

Sol stands there, pistol in hand, with the same odd look on his face, in front of the workbench, with the baseball scrapbook opened to the clipping about the hundreds of fans. Seth cannot imagine what Papa Sol might be thinking.

"Papa Sol?"

Papa Sol's right hand clutches the .38 delicately, as if he were holding a sparrow with a broken leg. Slowly, he brings his hand with the .38 in it toward his head and presses the barrel firmly against his right temple.

Seth is thinking about how baseball and passion are inextricably entwined, how the game can pull you in and take your breath away, how it can wrap you around its little finger and keep you there for life and maybe sometimes make you do things you don't mean to do.

"Papa Sol, it was just a game, *a stupid baseball game!*"

Papa Sol does not hear his grandson. Still the odd look on his face.

"Don't do it, Papa Sol! I love you *so much!* Papa Sol, please! *NOOOOOOO!*"

©

"*NOOOOOOO!*"

Seth Stein, slouched in the Naugahyde La-Z-Boy in his Cambridge town house, looks down at the pool of sweat that soaks his shirt.

How'd he get back home? It wasn't by clicking together his ruby slippers. This was all a dream, right? I mean, come on, *going back to visit 1951?*

But it seemed so real. He's sure he saw those sights and smelled those smells and heard those sounds, as if he were actually living them. And he *was* living them. Wasn't he? Plus, how could he have just made up all those details, like those humongous cars on Thirteenth Avenue and Papa Sol's funky old Philco radio and Uncle Miltie's shtick? And how do you explain the ball? Is he really in possession of *the* Bobby Thomson ball? Does it have magical powers? Did it really transport him back in time? Were Papa Sol's love for his grandson and passion for baseball drawing Seth back to him?

Seth is running on empty, but he can't stop himself from cogitating.

Did he actually witness the past? If so—like a religion scholar being granted a visit to Eden or a biology scholar being allowed to go back in time to witness the first lizard, the tuatara, walk on dry land—will it give him historical insights into his writing, his research, his teaching?

And what about Sol? Did he pull the trigger? Of course not, since he made it to seventy-six, last time Seth saw him. But what a scare. And who knew about that side of him? Suicide? Papa Sol? No way.

And why did Papa Sol withhold from him and Grandma Elsie the fact that he caught the famous ball Bobby hit? What about that suicidal episode, what was *that*? Who knew he even owned a gun? Did he ever mention it to Elsie? Why suicide? It was just a *ball*. Was it the humiliation, the frustration of not being able to share it with anyone—even his loved ones!—since he must have known no one would ever believe him? Was it his resentment of the greed and the lust for fame of other people? Or the shame of wanting, like them, to have his *own* fifteen minutes in the sun? Seth knows Sol didn't pull the trigger then, that night in the basement. But did he do it two years ago, which would explain his disappearance?

Were there in fact *two* Papa Sols? The Sol who lived by the rules of honesty and integrity and the Sol who bent the truth? The Sol who loved life and the Sol who pondered taking his own? The Sol who was hopeful and passionate and the Sol who was cynical and disillusioned? The sweet, soft Sol and the seething, smoldering Sol?

Why did Seth never see this side of Papa Sol, the side that was flawed? Did he only want to see the ideal version, or was that the only image Sol ever cared, or dared, to project?

And if Sol withheld information from his loved ones about catching the ball and owning the pistol and attempting suicide, what other little secrets did he hide from them and harbor deep within the recessed privacies of his soul?

What's more, historian Seth thinks, all this can't be true of just Papa Sol. Doesn't *everyone* have these hidden parts, these tucked-away compartments that no one else, including loved ones, can ever know? Doesn't this mean, historically speaking, that we can never know other people? That we can never know what motivates them deep inside and why they do what they do?

Seth struggles to get up, staggers to a pile of books on the floor at the other end of the study, rummages, brings a slender morocco-bound tome back to his chair. It is a volume of Schopenhauer, and he thumbs his way to the section titled "Aphorisms":

> *It is my belief that the events and characters narrated by history compare with reality more or less as the portraits of authors on frontispieces of books usually compare with the authors themselves, that is to say they do so only in outline, so that they bear only a faint similarity to them, or sometimes none at all.*

Seth's body is ready to pack it in, but his brain is still mulling over unresolved issues. Should he tell his sweetheart, Kate, about this, like he tells her about everything else? And also Grandma Elsie, when he visits her tomorrow? And Sammy, too? He wants to, wants to share his extraordinary journey to the past with them all, every last tidbit, but he knows he can't. Not yet. He still has questions, lots of them. And now that Pandora's box has been opened, he needs to find more answers, about Sol's life, about his disappearance into thin air. No, he must keep this to himself, for the time being, anyway.

Seth's bleary eyes glance at Papa Sol's opened yellowed

note. It remains cryptic, and the deciphering of its secrets will have to wait for another day.

Then at the ball. He closes the top of the box over it, shakes his head, sighs.

His eyes weigh about a ton and slam shut like the door to a cartoon dungeon. And as Morpheus whisks him away in his arms, Seth reviews the litany of recent events: the note . . . the ball . . . the tornado . . . the stroll down Thirteenth Avenue . . . the visit to 1270 . . . Papa Sol's carpentry . . . Uncle Miltie . . . Grandma Elsie in pj's . . . seeing his toddler father . . . the Polo Grounds . . . the Game . . . the Catch . . . the pistol to the temple . . .

It has been quite a day.

3

INCHES

YOUR LEGACY IS IN THE ATTIC.

Of the sixty-two words that make up the tantalizing note Solomon Stein had left behind, these are the six that especially haunt his grandson.

Seth sifts through artifacts collected by Grandma Elsie in three large cardboard boxes that have lain fallow for two years deep in the bowels of her attic. He has been up here for over an hour, searching for answers.

Stacks of yellowed letters, newspaper articles, old Red Sox programs, *Sports Illustrated*s and *Sporting News*es, assorted tools and carpentry paraphernalia, odd scraps of cherry and mahogany, baseball cards, a weather-beaten mitt from the thirties, a couple of poetry anthologies: all residua of Papa Sol's life that resonate with Seth, but nothing that suggests anything approaching a legacy.

Seth looks at his watch. It says one thirty, and it's only half an hour until his history class with those bushy-tailed freshmen. Gotta get a wiggle on.

He descends the nine stairs to the second floor, pops his head in the bedroom to check on Elsie. She is asleep, snoring, arms folded across her chest, her tranquil visage belying the terrible conflict she is still grappling with in her soul regarding her vanished husband.

Seth kisses her forehead, and Elsie parts her lips.

"Love you, *bubeleh,*" she whispers.

Seth wants to wake her up, blurt out everything. Tell her all about the wooden box and the ball and the tornado and Thirteenth Avenue and 1270 and the Hornet in the garage and young Sol working on the chair and Uncle Miltie and his toddler father and the Polo Grounds and the Catch and the pistol to the temple in the basement.

"Love you, too, Elfie."

◐

Seth and Jezebel bump their way toward Harvard Yard. Cottony snow gobs helicopter down from the heavens, and Seth is reciting in his head a poem that he adores, Paul Valéry's "Neige," which, when he was thirteen, Papa Sol had helped him memorize in the original French:

> *Quel pur désert tombé des ténèbres sans bruit*
> *Vint effacer les traits de la terre enchantée*
> *Sous cette ample candeur sourdement augmentée . . .*

Seth often recites this poem to himself when it is snowing. Finds it comforting, not only the gorgeous images of silence and whiteness, but also the sounds of the word clusters, of the dentals and the sibilants as they trip gallically off his tongue.

Flakes parachute onto Jeze's trunk, roof, and hood as she wheezes her way past the cemetery. When she spontaneously accelerates for no apparent reason, Seth smiles slyly, imagining that she always gets a wee bit nervous when she lumbers past a graveyard, especially on a frigid and snowy day.

Trooper that she is, Jeze slaloms around potholes and slams through moguls of slush that litter the length of Mt. Auburn Street, her weary wipers toiling at the speed of Vermont maple syrup to clear her windshield, but only barely, for Seth. Her battle-hardened, six-year-old Bridgestones manage a dainty left onto JFK, skid past Harvard Square and the Coop, slide a right onto Cambridge Street, then bear right, slipping onto Broadway, and eke out a harrowing, hard right onto Quincy Street, past the old Fogg Art Museum on the left, and—there, there's a spot!, a rara avis indeed, across from Lamont Library and only a few minutes' walk from Robinson Hall and the seminar room where Seth will soon be strutting his History stuff.

Ol' Jeze comes through once again. *You go, girl!*

On his way to Robinson, Seth's mind is not on the class he'll be leading in seven minutes. He is thinking about his urge to tell Kate and Grandma Elsie and Sammy about his visit to 1951. He wants to, but he can't, not yet. Can't, because he still needs answers, and how, to Papa Sol's mysteries. Can't, because he's still uncertain about whether it even happened.

The snow continues to descend. It is thick and lush and soft, as Cambridge snow can be at its breathtaking best, transforming Harvard Yard from weasel to ermine.

As Seth approaches Robinson Hall, the rectangular, nondescript home of the History department tucked away at 35 Quincy Street in the northeast corner of the Yard, he re-recites a phrase from the Valéry poem that captures the regal white expanse spread out before him: *Sous cette ample candeur,* "Beneath this ample innocence." He loves parsing words, reveling in the unraveling of the connotative ambiguity of language, and he turns over in his mind the linguistic possibilities of the deceptively simple word *candeur:* innocence . . . purity . . . whiteness . . .

So why the hell can't I figure out Papa Sol's note?

Up the three steps of the main entrance, inside Robinson now, shake the snow off the Red Wings, unzip the parka, off with the Red Sox cap. On his way up the first flight of stairs, Seth puts his right hand instinctively into his right pants pocket, expecting to find three or four coins, which he is habitually fond of twiddling, like Bogie with the steel balls when he played Queeg. Instead, his fingertips discover a piece of paper. Like a blind man, he palpates the object in an attempt to guess its identity. Its texture is more like soft, thin cardboard, thicker than regular paper. It is smooth, no bumps or raised letters. About an inch wide, maybe three, four inches long, serrated edge on only one end. Doesn't ring the slightest bell, but his curiosity is sure piqued.

It's almost two by Seth's watch and he doesn't have the time to futz around with the little guessing game, so he yanks the object out of his pocket.

Gadzooks.

He reads the writing on the artifact, every last letter, top to bottom and side to side. Then reads it again, just to be sure. Nope, no doubt about it.

RAIN CHECK . . . UPPER RES. SEAT . . . **$2.00** . . . **N.Y. GIANTS** Baseball Club . . . **POLO GROUNDS** . . . GAME NO. **PO-2** . . . **PLAY-OFF GAME** . . . NOT REDEEMABLE FOR CASH . . . See Other Side For Conditions . . . **Play-off Game** . . . In the event of a postponement this coupon will admit the holder to the game numbered hereon. Not good if detached from RAIN CHECK . . . Upper Reserved Seat Est. price $1.67-Tax Paid .33 **$2.00** . . . Right reserved to revoke license granted by this ticket by refunding purchase price . . .

*Horace C. Stoneham*President

Seth is immobilized right in the middle of the staircase, bustling students flickering around him in both directions like an animated army of ants circumventing a dead twig.

Could it be? Was I actually there? I must've been . . . how else . . . this ticket . . .

Huh?

But this is clearly impossible. Patently absurd. No way, Jose. A visit back to 1951, my ass.

But the ticket stub?

Dazed, Seth makes his way to the seminar room, struggling to resolve the troubling paradox but knowing that he's got to postpone sorting it out, that, after all, he's got responsibilities—

"Ladies and gentlemen . . ."

"Dr. Stein . . ."

"Today we're going to discuss . . ."

For the very first time in his professorial career, the usually eloquent, personable, and glib Seth Stein is an inarticulate imbecile, a babbling buffoon at a loss for words. He has forgotten his lesson plan, even the gist of the discussion he has prepared for today. He has forgotten how to speak.

". . . to . . . to . . . discuss . . ."

A pen clatters on the floor of the classroom. Hands fidget. Fingers play with parka zippers. Notebook pages rustle. Seth pulls himself together.

"... to discuss whether History is a truly noble study or total bullshit."

The nine freshmen sitting around the rectangular wooden table in the seminar room are taken aback, momentarily stunned, their collective breathing halted in mid-exhalation. It is not Seth's colloquial, student-friendly language that they find shocking. No, they are used to it, in fact, find it refreshing compared to the starched, patrician airs of some of the formal, full-professorial Cantabrigian characters they've taken classes from. It's just that they were expecting a lively discussion of the JFK assassination this afternoon, not this open-ended, abstract topic that seems risibly ambitious, way too much to handle in a paltry fifty minutes.

Dr. Stein, on the other hand, is *inspired.* Having found himself in a pedagogical pickle, inarticulate and trapped deep in his own backfield, he is having to improvise, to juke and change direction and evade tacklers and find a hole and break into the didactic open field for a long gain. He has succeeded in ad-libbing his way into a brand-new, unplanned discussion topic, one that has been gestating in his thoughts, its genesis in his purported trip back in time.

This is what teaching is all about, Seth thinks.

"So then, who wants to initiate the discussion?"

Dead silence. The freshmen are still in shock. Even Stephanie Lowell, who *always* has her hand up.

"All right, guys, I see you're not gonna make this any easier on me. Well, looks like I'll have to be the one to start things off. Let's see. Okay, let's begin with a quote. Hmmm. All right, I've got it. It's from that eminent historian Alfred North Whitehead. Ol' Al [*assorted titters*] once said, 'The real history does not get written, because it's not in people's brains but in their nerves and vitals.' Now, what do you think he meant by *that*?"

A pause, then Old Faithful Ms. Lowell raises her hand and erupts.

"Well, I think that ol' Al [*more titters*] might've meant that, y'know, the history that we read about is all about what people in the past are thinking, but we don't find out what they're truly feeling. I mean, don't actions usually stem from emotions rather than thoughts? But we never study *feelings*!"

Stephanie, a perky, cheeky, smart-as-a-whip blonde from nearby Natick (Seth thinks she looks like Betty from the Archie comic books), sits back in her chair, quite taken with her response.

"Very good, Stephanie," Seth says. "A nice start. But what do you mean by 'thinking' and 'feeling'? How can we know only what people think and not what they feel? And don't we sometimes know what they're feeling and not what they're thinking?"

Another pause, but Josh Greenfield, who's barely said a word all term, knifes in with, "I'm not sure I really know the difference between thinking and feeling."

The class guffaws heartily as one.

Josh retorts, "No . . . I mean . . . I *know* the difference, but, like, how can they really be separated? Sometimes people from History perform intellectual actions that are the result of their emotions, and sometimes they act with emotions that come from their thinking process, so how can we know which is which, really?"

"Well, you make a good point," Seth says. "But what do you think ol' Al meant by people's 'nerves and vitals'? Why do you think he said that *this* history doesn't get written?"

Neofeminist Libby Frank, the mousy Emily Litella look-alike sitting to Seth's immediate left, pipes up. "It seems to me that we can never really know what people are feeling in their gut, in their viscera, because that is an inner place that doesn't give out its secrets. That's why History only records man's intellectual acts. Now *women*—"

"Okay," Seth interrupts respectfully, "let's not get too political here. That's a good thought, Libby. I think ol' Al would agree with you on that. So that begs the question, why don't we ever get the 'real scoop'? Why don't we ever find out what people in the past are truly feeling? Is it because feelings are short-lived? Are they impossible to 'record,' as opposed to facts or data or events?"

Silence. Deep thinking.

Jamaal Crosby, a cross between Barack Obama and Maury Wills who's been giving his best impression of Rodin's *Le Penseur* until now, speaks. "I think that life is pretty complicated and that every important moment just gets boiled down to facts. Not what people are feeling deep down, but just the kernel of what really happened."

Bingo.

The mother lode. Just when Seth was thinking the discussion was losing a little steam, it's good ol' Jamaal to the rescue.

"Excellent, Jamaal," Seth says. "An example that comes to mind from baseball history is the sixth game of the '86 Series."

Inured to Seth's use of the National Pastime as a pedagogical tool, the students know what's coming and exhale a sarcastic collective groan.

"Sure, we know that the game ended 6–5 Mets and that Billy Buckner booted Mookie's grounder and that Ray Knight scored the winning run, but what about Buckner's nerves and vitals? A big chunk of the history of this game may never be known as long as Billy remains a recluse in

Idaho and refuses to give any more interviews. The true impact and meaning of the game may well remain in his gut and someday end up buried six feet under or strewn in the wind. Now, can anyone think of an example or two outside of baseball to corroborate Jamaal's theory?"

Maria Lopez accepts the challenge. "What about the JFK assassination? After all, we were supposed to talk about that today."

"Yeah, right on!"

"Hoo-ha!"

"You tell 'im, Maria!"

"Yes, Maria?" Seth asks, attempting to restore order.

"Well," Maria continues, "let's think about it. What was Jackie feeling when she climbed onto the back of the limo? What was Oswald feeling when he squeezed the trigger? What was the guy on the grassy knoll feeling when he saw Kennedy's brains exploding out? What were all those people in Dealey Plaza feeling when they witnessed the tragedy? What was the whole country feeling when they lost their president? What was the CIA feeling when they cooked up the whole thing? I don't think we'll ever know the totality of the real event that happened. All we've got is the Zapruder tape, some newsreels, the bullshit Warren Report, and a bunch of conflicting theories. Just artifacts, brain work. No nerves, no vitals."

"That's the ticket, Maria," Seth responds. "Now we're cooking with gas. Any other examples from the past?"

The right arms of all nine students shoot straight up around the table, a picket fence of unbridled enthusiasm.

"Bron?"

Bronson Larrabee IV, a shy, lanky hobbledehoy and the fourth generation of Larrabees to attend Harvard, clears his throat. "Umm, how about the Civil War? What comes to us as history is mostly numbers and places and names: six hundred twenty thousand dead, Fort Sumter, Antietam, Appomattox, Lincoln, Grant, Lee. But what were the soldiers feeling? What about the actual pain and misery that went down? And the soldiers' widows? What were *they* feeling? And Lincoln, how must *he* have felt, with all his internal conflict and the tough decisions he had to make?"

"Wow, Bron. Well said! In fact, you basically expressed the same thought as Walt Whitman, maybe the greatest poet America has ever produced."

The students applaud for Bron. Their version of a gold star.

Seth rifles through his briefcase, fumbles through a few folders, plucks out a yellow index card with a quote on it. He fondles the words as if delivering one of Hamlet's soliloquies:

> *Future years will never know the seething hell and the black infernal background of the countless minor scenes and interiors . . . of the Secession war; and it is best they should not—the real war will never get in the books.*

Seth is having fun. How lovely to see the kids engaged like this. But he's sorely tempted at this point to talk to them about what precipitated this discussion in the first place, what has been occupying nearly his every thought. He wants to share with them his visit to the past, just like he wants to share it with Kate and Elsie and Sammy. Bat it around a bit, see what their take on it is. Talk to them about how he was privileged to go back in time, to smell and hear and see History, to feel the nerves and vitals of the denizens of 1951.

Not yet.

"So," Seth proffers to his attentive sponges, "this all leads to the query I posed at the outset about History. Noble study? Or bullshit? That is, is studying the past a challenge to us, an opportunity to imagine what happened, to interpret what happened, to conclude what happened? Or is it just too vague and too superficial to have any real meaning? Mind you, I personally am planning to spend the rest of my professional life digging up, studying, thinking about, and teaching this very bullshit."

A roar of laughter explodes from the students.

The discussion sails along like this—stimulating, spirited, opinionated, thoughtful, inclusive—until the bell rings.

To Seth's surprise, the students rise in unison and spontaneously give him a rousing standing ovation, a phenomenon generally reserved for the end of the final meeting of the term.

This is what teaching is all about, Seth thinks.

(⊙)

Kate Richman has just eaten a canary. Or so her feline smirk seems to indicate.

The source of her mirth is a delicious evening to remember with serious boyfriend Seth Stein: drinks (Sea Breeze for her, Balvenie for him), session of passionate lovemaking, romantic dinner for two (candlelight; Mozart, James Taylor, Gino Paoli; cream of broccoli soup, Caesar salad from scratch, killer chicken piccata with basmati rice; bottle of Sancerre).

Seth is still digesting the magnificent repast Kate has served up. He loves it that she is such a spectacular cook and is so proud of her professional trajectory in the field of haute cuisine, working her way up from lowly *commis* to *saucier* to *chef de partie* to, just recently, *sous-chef*. And of the fact that she's worked at some of Boston's finest culinary establishments, including Hammersley's Bistro, Aujourd'hui, L'Espalier, The Four Seasons, and Silks, in Lowell.

He examines one of the walls in Kate's place, where two framed diplomas hang:

DIPLÔME DE CUISINE
LE CORDON BLEU

CERTIFICAT
DE PERFECTIONNEMENT PROFESSIONNEL
DE CUISINE LE CORDON BLEU

Between the diplomas is a framed picture of Kate in chef's hat, posing between Chef Didier Chantefort and Directeur Académique Sylvie Sofi Alarcon.

Seth looks at Kate, his heart bursting with pride and love. But now's not the perfect time to pop the question: There's the heart disease thing and the specter of his horrific divorce still lurking even after six years and the issue of investing once again in a long-term commitment. But when the time is right, he thinks—

Maybe *now's* the perfect time, thinks Kate, who up to now has not said a peep regarding the *m* word to her best friend and lover. Now's perfect, because they'll find a way to make it work despite all his issues and they love each other so much, fer chrissakes, and Love Conquers All, doesn't it?

She is curled up in her favorite rocking chair—comfy in her red Daffy Duck pajamas, blue terry robe, and fuzzy, fleece-lined yellow slippers—and gazes at Seth, who's putting on his Red Wings and getting ready to return to his town house. He often stays over at Kate's, but he's got a meeting tomorrow with his department chairman and pressing work to do on the book and needs to be up late into the wee hours with his papers and his laptop.

Seth has no desire in the world to leave. He's feeling so good, between the terrific class with the bushy-tailed freshmen and the evening with Kate, and she's looking so fine just now across from him—with that Rita Hayworth hair and those Elizabeth Taylor eyes and that Ann-Margret smile and that Brigitte Bardot body—and it's still snowing and the snow is so gorgeous and it's so cozy in here.

"I had a real *swell* time tonight, sister," Seth says, with his Bogie accent.

"Me, too," Lauren Bacall coos.

"The piccata was poifect, just enough lemon—"

"Seriously, Seth, you were amazing tonight. Where'd all that energy come from?"

"Dunno. Had a great seminar with the kids today, did I tell you?"

"Only three times."

"Kate?"

"That's me. What?"

"I was thinking, naaah—"

"*What?*"

Kate is thinking maybe this is it, the big moment she's been waiting for.

"Well, would you ever keep a secret from me?"

"Huh?" unhappy camper Kate blurts.

"I mean, do you tell me *everything*?"

"Why do you ask?"

"Just wondering. You know how I'm wondering all the time. Well?"

Seth employs all his inner strength to avoid spilling the beans concerning his 1951 visit with Papa Sol.

Kate employs all her inner strength to avoid clenching her teeth and rushing into the kitchen to get a rolling pin so she can bop Seth one and knock some sense into him.

"Well, I don't know," Kate says. "I suppose there are things I don't talk about."

"Like what?"

"Oh, maybe girl things, you know, stuff you might not be especially interested in. Or maybe stuff you don't need to be thinking about. Nothing *big*. I'm sure there are little things I keep to myself, but that's normal, right?"

"I guess. Yeah, pretty normal. I'm sure all couples have their little secrets."

"Seth?"

"Yep?"

"Is there something you'd like to tell me?"

"No, sweetie pie. I promise. Just wondering out loud."

For now, the agendas remain hidden, the talking is over, and the two lovebirds are reduced to chirping.

"I love you, Seth Stein."

"I love you, Kate Richman."

Seth plants a kiss on Kate's warm, full lips, gives her a big bear hug.

"Seth honey, what's that stain on your sleeve?"

○

Kate's place is only ten minutes from Seth's, and he loves the walk between the two abodes. Snow blankets most of his Red Sox cap, including the big red **B** above the blue peak. He jokes to himself that he is now walking through the streets of Chicago's South Side, because he is wearing a white Sox cap. Funny. Well, not *that* funny.

Seth moseys down Oxford, past Annenberg Hall, then cuts through the Yard, past Thayer, University, and Weld, then Widener Library, and through the gate at Wigglesworth. *Wigglesworth* is his favorite word in the English language. Right up there with *haberdasher.*

He is having an imaginary conversation with Papa Sol.

"You know, I haven't told a soul about the ball, not my students, not Gram, not Sammy, not even Kate—"

"That's my Setharoo."

"Not yet, that is. I'm still looking for answers. Then—"

"Well, I'm sure you'll do what's right. Man's gotta do—"

"Not that I'm not tempted. After all, you *did* leave us without a word, so why the hell should I keep all your dirty laundry to myself? You sorta gave up your right to my loyalty when you left—"

"Now, that's a trifle harsh, Setharoo. Didn't we have some good times? Didn't you feel the love?"

Again, the chicken-bone lump.

"You *know* I did, Papa Sol. And that's why I'm clamming up until I find out more. But it better be soon, because I can't keep mum too much longer."

Terminating the dialogue, Seth turns left onto Mass. Ave., then straight onto Harvard Street, and now the key's in the door.

He can barely feel his appendages as he makes a pot of *café filtre,* takes off his Red Wings, and dials Sammy's number on his cell phone.

"Samaroo, that you?"

"Nope, wrong again, Sherlock. It's his mom."

"Hey, Julie."

"Hey, yourself."

"Listen, as long as I have you on the line, would you mind telling me why I haven't heard from my son in almost a week?"

"What am I, his *keeper*? Sammy's twelve, and he's a big boy. I think he can make this kind of decision all by his lonesome."

Seth's cheeks become flushed, his lips tighten. Lovely facial reminders of how his ex is still a genius at pushing his buttons.

"Well, Julie, do me a big favor and, if you can possibly force yourself, try not to say anything too mean about me to him. I've spent a big chunk of my life bringing that kid up and giving him my love, and I'd appreciate it if you refrained from driving any pesky wedges between him and me."

"You wanna speak to Sam? I don't really have the time to listen to this—"

"Yeah, put him on."

"Dad?"

"Hey, Samaroo! How's life?"

"Not bad. And you?"

"Thanks for asking. Pretty good, actually. Working hard on the book and Kate is cookin' up a storm and next year I got a feeling the Bosox are gonna win the Series *again*!"

"That'd be cool."

"So I haven't heard from you in a while. Whassup?"

"Nothin' much. Soccer's going good—"

"Going *well* . . ."

"Yeah, whatever. And school's hard, but I'm doing pretty goo . . . *well*."

"That's my Samaroo! Hey listen, how'd you like to go see the Revs play soccer down in Foxborough?"

"Awesome. But I'll have to ask Mom first—"

"*Sammy?* Remember what we discussed last time? We don't need to ask your mom's permission for this. Anyway, I gotta run. Think about it, and I'll call you again in a couple of days. Deal?"

"Yeah, deal."

"Okay then. I love you—"

"Love you, too, Dad."

That's so damn sad, Seth reflects as he closes the phone. What a great kid Sammy is and how great we were together, just like Papa Sol and I were. But ever since Julie and I split to ring in the millennium, things aren't quite the same with us. He barely ever opens up to me anymore, like he used to. She must be telling him shit. . . .

Seth removes his guitar from its hard black case, moves the capo up to cover the fourth fret. Nothing like a few good riffs to lift the spirit and warm the cockles.

Sitting on his hard-backed guitar chair, with his Martin 000-28EC resting on his right thigh, Seth is in heaven. The thinness of her neck is just right for the lithe but short fingers of his left hand as they dart up and down the frets. Between sips of java, he soothes body and soul with the gentle, rhythmic back-and-forth of his right thumb as he Travis-picks his way through a medley of old bluesy licks, covering for Mississippi John Hurt, Rev. Gary Davis, Mark Spoelstra, Robert Johnson, Doc Watson, Dave Van Ronk.

Cocaine's for horses, not for men
They tell me it'll kill me but they won't say when
Cocaine, run all 'round my brain . . .

He gives up the double-thumb a while, does some assorted fingerpicking, comes upon Leigh Harline and Ned

Washington's classic 1940 "When You Wish Upon a Star"
in his computer mind. One of his all-time favorite tunes.
Having trouble working out the chord sequence, though.
What the hell comes after the G and G variations in the
second half of the second bar? D? Nope. D minor? Crap.
Hmmm . . . *Aha!* Good ol' F sharp diminished.

Another sip of joe, and Seth looks down at the right
sleeve of his shirt. Sees a thick yellow-brown stain, the one
Kate noticed a while ago. Has no clue where it came from.
Takes a whiff. Yuck. Smell is familiar, can't quite put a
name to it.

After some mental effort, Seth identifies the mystery
stain as mustard. But he hates mustard. Never eats the
stuff. Another quick sniff, and he deduces that it is, in fact,
ballpark mustard.

Jumpin' Jehosaphat.

First the ticket stub, now the mustard stain. *Did I really
live in History?*

Out of the corner of his eye, Seth spies Papa Sol's
wooden box. He hasn't noticed it since he first opened it
up the other night, but now that it's got his attention, it is
beckoning to him, and he becomes a moth to its candle.

Gotta get to my book, but first this. Just a quick gander.

Sinking into his La-Z-Boy, Seth opens the top of the
case, and there it is. The very ball Bobby Thomson cranked
into the stands and into Papa Sol's nimble left hand.

Seth ponders the significance of this silly stitched-up
hunk of horsehide. What baseball meant to Papa Sol, what
it means to him, to America. Baseball, Papa Sol, History—
all threads that connect themselves to one another and to
Seth, like the very stitches on the ball that hold the flaps of
horsehide together. So if he did travel back in time, was
there a reason for it? Baseball, Papa Sol, History. A mantra

that suggests that maybe there is some strange, powerful karma in the ball that is pulling him back, allowing him to discover secrets that until now have remained concealed.

As he eyes the ball, Seth is filled with melancholy. He is sad that Papa Sol was never around to see his love for Kate blossom, to see the Red Sox finally win the Series, to see Sammy's age turn double digits. How proud his grandfather would have been.

Seth picks up the baseball and, onto its surface, slaps his separated index and middle fingers, a serpent's tongue darting across the two parallel rows of crimson stitching. His thumb cradles the ball's underbelly, and the three fingers, as if in a hypnotic trance, place themselves robotically in the curveball position. The same curve that Ralph Branca never threw to Bobby Thomson. The same one that, had Branca thrown it, might have made him the hero and Bobby the goat, instead of the other way around. On what a slender thread the vicissitudes of History hang, Seth thinks. How many major events have occurred that resulted from the age-old baseball vagaries: a bad bounce here, the wrong pitch there? History, like baseball: a game of inches.

Seth rotates his hand with the ball in it clockwise, slowly but without releasing it, just like that curve Branca never threw.

Whoa.

Seth knows the drill by now: The room is spinning, now faster, and the Oz music—*Dah-de-lah-de-lah*—and the feeling of calm and the Beatles' riff and now the Fantastical Historical Slide Show.

This time, the chronological people and events passing before his eyes are different but no less fascinating. The invention of the abacus and the founding of Byzantium and Siddhartha founds Buddhism and the Peloponnesian War and Christ is born and Charlemagne dies and Erik the Red settles Greenland and Jamestown is settled and Galileo recants Copernicus and the French Revolution and Booth shooting Lincoln and the Scopes "Monkey Trial" and Churchill, FDR, and Stalin at Yalta and the Korean War and John Glenn orbiting the earth . . .

And the final burst of the Beatles' riff and the rousing, raucous, brash, clashing, strident, high-pitched, piercing, trumpety climax. And the tornado grinds to a halt. And Seth is deposited gently on the ground. It is no longer 2006.

☾

It is 1962.

Seth knows it is, because he is in a kitchen on one of whose walls hangs an Official 1962 San Francisco Giants Calendar. The exposed page features a color photo of Giants manager Alvin Dark sporting a stupid-ass grin, his arm around the waist of one of his star pitchers, Juan Marichal. On the bottom half of the page is the month of October.

Alone in the immaculate kitchen, Seth also knows that he is in Sol and Elsie's Berkeley home, the one they moved into in '58 to be with the Giants, the one he moved into in '76 to be with them.

He instantly recognizes this room where he spent so many magical hours during his formative years. And the homey, old-fashioned look, rather spiffy in its time: pink stove, pastel blue cabinets, pine paneling, Formica counters, turquoise electric skillet, manual juicer, venetian blinds.

He crosses the kitchen to the bay window, peers out.

Wow.

Seth recollects how breathtaking the view was, and still

is. He's way up in the hills, the sky is clear and black and gorgeous. He gazes out at the glorious San Francisco Bay, first at Alcatraz and the Golden Gate Bridge, then pans counterclockwise, to the twinkling lights of the city, and there's Coit Tower and the Bay Bridge and, to his immediate left, the UC Berkeley campus with the Campanile—

"Goddam Jints!" Solomon Stein spews from an adjacent room.

"Sweetie, it's just a game," Elsie says, in a lame effort to console.

With no caution, Seth leaves the kitchen, confident in the knowledge that he is once again invisible and inaudible.

In the living room, he sees thirty-four-year-old Papa Sol, thirty-three-year-old Grandma Elfie, and the devilishly handsome fourteen-year-old barefoot lad with the long mop, that must be . . .

Simon Stein.

In the background, a stereo system receiver plays a Del Shannon LP.

Papa Sol has sprouted a beard since Seth's visit to the younger version of the carpenter, but the eleven years between visits have treated his grandfather kindly. Not a trace of gray, not an ounce heavier, not a wrinkle on his face.

"Just a game? Maybe for you, Else, but the Jints and I, we go back a long ways."

"You tell 'er, Pop," Seth's father goads. The lad is wearing a Willie Mays T-shirt, a black Giants baseball cap with orange interlocking **SF** on the front, and frayed jeans with impressive holes on each knee.

"Goddam Giants," Sol grumbles. "It's the World Series, against the Yanks, two games apiece, the big fifth game, tied 2–2 into the eighth, Jack Sanford's pitching for us, he's gone seven and a third with ten Ks, just sailing along, and pitching against Ralph Terry, who's oh-for-four lifetime in Series decisions. And what does ol' Jack do? Throws a gopher ball, a three-run job, to Tommy Tresh, *a damn rookie!* So now we're down in the Series 3–2, in a hole. Goddam Giants! Damn Yankees!"

"I know, honey pie," Elsie consoles. "But think of it this way. Look at what this country is going through now, what with the Cold War and all that racial trouble. And you're worrying about the Giants losing a ball game?"

Del Shannon is singing "Runaway," and Seth is feeling like one. Like he has run away from home to visit a strange, faraway land. The strangest part of which is the vision, right here and right now in this Berkeley living room, of the father he barely remembers, the dad he never got to know, the pop he never had the chance to bond with. Seth can't take his eyes off this fourteen-year-old kid of whose loins he is the product, this adolescent who gave him life, started him off in the right direction, and then was snuffed out just like that by a goddam faulty airplane engine, robbing him of the joy of seeing his only child grow up and flourish.

An exquisite shiver, starting from Seth's nape, traverses the length of his spine and doesn't stop until it reaches the tips of all ten toes.

Simon Stein is seated in his rocking chair, facing Papa Sol on the couch.

"Okay, Simaroo, you ready?"

Sol's son nods.

"Okay then, here goes . . ."

Solomon Stein looks at Seth's father intently, and the tension builds through his silence. And then: *"Chuck!"*

Simon leaps forward out of his chair, propelled by passion. He assumes Chuck Hiller's compressed stance in the batter's box and then, with his imaginary bat, pretends to lay down a perfect drag bunt. Then back to his chair to await further instructions.

"*Orlando!*" Sol barks.

The fourteen-year-old lunges forward, coils up as Orlando Cepeda would, and explodes into the first sacker's powerful swing, eyes gleaming with ferocity. Then back to his chair.

Seth's mouth is crowbarred open by the thrill of seeing his dad perform this baseball pantomime, the same family tradition Sol continued with Seth during his formative and adolescent years.

Grandma Elfie beams in the background.

The pace quickens, Papa Sol's rapid-fire commands propelling Simon Stein out of his chair and into a succession of baseball silent movie clips, then back again to the chair.

"*Tom!*"

Simon crouches in Tom Haller's catching position.

"*Willie!*"

Simon mimics Willie McCovey's august and imposing left-handed batter's stance.

"No, the *other* Willie!"

Simon giggles, then, his back to Sol, reproduces to perfection Willie Mays's miracle, behind-the-back catch against Vic Wertz in the '54 Series vs. Cleveland.

Seth is taking all this History in, his fond memories of the same madcap exercise he used to perform for Papa Sol reconstituting themselves. The parallel between him and Simon Stein fills his heart as he watches the father he never knew sharing the same passion for baseball he knows so well.

"Jimmy!"

Jim Davenport leaps to snare a ball at the hot corner.

"Jose!"

Shortstop Pagan ranges to his right, backhands a grounder deep in the hole, throws to Cepeda for the out.

"Jack!"

Righty pitcher Sanford delivers a corker.

"Billy!"

Lefty pitcher O'Dell (or Pierce, take your pick) paints the corner.

"Juan!"

Seth can't help himself and joins in on the action, his invisible body shadowing Simon's physical one from behind, his movements replicating those of his father, as if the two were performing some weird baseball version of that virtuoso dance number between Gene Kelly and Jerry the Mouse in the 1945 film *Anchors Aweigh.*

Two Juan Marichals show off their famous high leg kicks.

"Don!"

A pair of Don Larsens execute their no-windup deliveries.

"Stu!"

Stu Miller and his twin brother are blown off the mound.

Sol gives up, Elsie breaks up, Simon cracks up, Seth wells up.

Del Shannon is singing "Hats Off to Larry" on the stereo. Sol perks up, picks up his cap from the couch, winks at his son, and he and Simon do a vaudeville shtick Sol has concocted, a spirited dance step featuring the removal and violent shaking of their Giants caps. Chortling hysterically, the two hoofers disappear into the kitchen.

The same routine he used to do with me, Seth thinks, his face flushed.

When father and son return to the living room, Sol has something important to impart.

"Now, Simaroo, I want to talk to you about hatred."

"Sol! You—"

"Elsie," Sol says, with a sweet sternness. "The boy needs to hear this."

A winking Papa Sol speaks in his familiar loving, mock-serious voice.

"Well, son, you know I would never teach you to hate another human being, right?"

"'Course not, Dad," Simon says.

"And you know that there's a strict rule around this house: *Love thy neighbor.* Right?"

"Right!" Simon agrees, winking at his mom.

"Well, Simaroo, that's still the rule, but every rule has an exception, and I'm gonna tell you right now what that exception is."

"And what might *that* be?" Simon, playing along, asks, with mock innocence.

"The exception to *Love thy neighbor* is . . . *It's okay to hate the Yankees!*"

Simon smiles, but not quite as broadly as his son.

"Now, let me make it perfectly clear that this is altogether different from hating a single person, which is not a good thing. On the contrary, this is about hating a team, the baddest, awfulest, terriblest, disgustingest team that ever lived. It's about hating a team that has tortured, taunted, teased, and tormented our beloved Giants for lo these many years. Why, they beat us in the last four World Series they played us, in '23, '36, '37, and '51. And the one in '23 was the very first of the nineteen they've won. The last time we beat them was all the way back in '22, *which was forty years ago!* Even the Dodgers (we hate *them,* too!) beat those Yanks in the '55 Series, just to rub our noses in it. And now, we're playing those hated Yankees again in the Series, and they're up three games to two and we simply *cannot* allow them to beat us again!"

Papa Sol is spent from his mock vituperation but continues on, requiring an exclamation point to terminate his little fatherly diatribe.

"So, Simon, my son, repeat after me: 'I hate the Yankees, I hate the Yankees. . . .' "

Simon joins in the chorus, in this baseball rite of passage, and is officially endoctrinated into the OSYHAA, the Official Stein Yankee-Hating Association of America.

Of which a glowing Seth has been a loyal and longtime member in good standing.

Seth is taking it all in, thrilled to be back in the lap of History once again. On the heels of the ticket stub and the mustard stain from his last trip back in time, he thinks, maybe this *is* real. He rubs his eyes to wipe off the moisture . . .

Ⓒ

. . . then opens them to a postcard of a Northern California day, crisp, fogless, smogless, cloudless, deep blue skies, the comforting yet penetrating rays of a late afternoon sun. The kind of perfect baseball afternoon you'd imagine was in the back of Jack Norworth's mind when, in 1908, he penned the innocent lyrics to "Take Me Out to the Ball Game."

Seth is at another baseball park from bygone days, but it's not the physical appearance, like at the Polo Grounds, that gives away its identity. Not the configuration, not the irregularity, not the dimensions or the clock or the score-board or the bull pens. No, it is the simple fact that on this particular afternoon, the sun is brilliant and it is seventy degrees with a humidity of 58 percent, yet nearly everyone in the stands is bundled up in jackets or parkas or some sort of outer protection from the swirling winds and the bitterly chill air.

The stadium that lodges these 43,948 would-be skiers can be none other than the home to the San Francisco Gi-ants, the ballpark that hosted the 1961 All-Star Game where a gust of wind blew Stu Miller off the mound, the venue nicknamed "North Pole" and "Cave of the Winds" and where during a Mets BP in '63 another gust picked up the batting cage and dropped it sixty feet six inches away onto the mound, the park that witnessed both the Beatles' final concert on 8/29/66 and the Loma Prieta 7.1 earthquake, which disrupted Game 3 of the '89 Giants-A's World Se-ries, the enclosure named after the indigenous wading bird of the long-billed curlew family, the arena absolutely unfit for the playing of baseball games: Candlestick Park.

The 'Stick!

Seth is sitting in a box seat down the first-base line, right behind the dugout. To his left are his Papa Sol and his father.

He is putting two and two together: Candlestick Park, windy autumn day in 1962, and look, the New York Yan-kees are on the field. There's Clete Boyer 6, Tony Kubek 10, Bobby Richardson 1, and Moose Skowron 14 tossing grounders. On the outfield bluegrass are Tommy Tresh 15, Mickey Mantle 7, Roger Maris 9, left to right. Then Elston Howard 32 behind the dish and Ralph Terry 23 on the mound.

His eyes scan the outfield scoreboard:

N.Y.   000 010 000
S.F.   000 000 00

Yep, it's the bottom of the ninth of one of the most thrilling World Series games ever, the deciding Game 7 of the '62 Fall Classic between Alvin Dark's Jints and Ralph Houk's Bronx Bombers.

"Papa Sol—," Seth says, turning to his left, then realizing that the ability to communicate and be heard isn't in his job description.

The swirling wind compels Simon Stein to zip up his black-and-orange Giants jacket all the way.

"Gettin' chilly, are we now?" Sol asks.

Proud Simon shakes his head and smiles. Proud Seth does the same.

"Hey, getcha hot dogs, getcha franks right heah," a young vendor shouts down the row of seats.

Sol looks at Simon, who nods.

"Two dogs right here, my man," Sol shouts.

Invisible Seth is famished and nearly yells out, "Make that three!" But by now he knows the drill.

Bills are handed down the aisle, wieners and coins are passed up the aisle, and father and son happily munch.

"Y'know, Simaroo, the great actor Humphrey Bogart, good ol' Bogie, once said, 'A hot dog at the ball game beats roast beef at the Ritz.' Yessirree Bob, there's nothing like it on God's green earth."

Simon looks up. "What's the Ritz, Dad?"

"Oh, just some fancy-shmancy hotel."

Seth's dad buys the explanation and stuffs his mouth with dog. A wayward clump of mustard dots the tip of his nose, and he and Papa Sol surrender to momentary hilarity.

While Ralph Terry takes his final warm-up tosses on the

mound, Seth takes in his surroundings. Unlike at the '51 game, the historian senses a distinct feeling of positive energy. At ball games, he is thinking, there are certainly always passion, rooting, partisanship, raw emotions. But whereas in '51 you could feel the animus and rawness right down to the fans' viscera, here, there is something more mellow. Part of it has to do with being in California. Part of it is that then the Jints were playing the hated Dodgers, and now they are playing the somewhat less hated Yanks.

But the biggest part is that despite the challenges and bad news of this past year—the U-2 incident, the Cold War, the Cuban Missile Crisis, civil war in the Congo, racial tension in the South, Rachel Carson's *Silent Spring,* and the death of Marilyn Monroe—there is hope in the air at the start of this new decade. A young and vibrant JFK is in office, inspiring American youth and promising to put a man on the moon by decade's end. John Glenn has orbited the earth. Americans don't have Richard Nixon to kick around anymore. Technology has grown wings, producing innovations like Telstar 1, digitized voice circuits, the first computer game, and sugar-free soft drinks. This year has also witnessed new hope for baseball, with the birth of the first two National League expansion teams, the New York Mets and the Houston Colt .45s. So all in all, everyone's happy to be here at this time and this place, all 43,948 of these carefree fans, and why not?

The wind is whipping and swirling in from dead center instead of the usual left-center. The sun's rays are beating down on Seth's face and neck, reflecting the intensity of the action on the field. Feels to him like that scene on the beach in Camus's *L'Étranger* where the merciless, glaring sun strikes the forehead of absurdist hero Meursault like a knife.

Solomon Stein and Simon Stein take synchronous chomps out of their hot dogs. Papa Sol takes a gulp of his Bud, leans back in his seat, chants under his breath, "I hate the Yankees. . . ." Simon joins in, also sotto voce.

So far, there has not been much for either Solomon or Simon Stein to get hopped up about, except for Willie Mc-Covey's triple in the seventh. But the lad is still tickled to be here, and Papa Sol has taught him well. Taught him that even if you don't score runs, a game can still be exciting, because it's close and anything can happen. Speaking of which, this is the last of the ninth of the deciding game of a World Series with Terry pitching, the very same Terry who blew it in the last of the ninth of the deciding Series game exactly two years ago by giving up that gopher ball to Pittsburgh Pirates second baseman Bill Mazeroski and would he do it again or be the hero this time?

Seth is also tickled to be here and to witness History once again and to see his very own father having such a swell time with his Papa Sol.

Yanks catcher Howard pegs the ball to shortstop Kubek, and Seth's eyes wander back to the scoreboard. Eight and a half innings played, one run scored in the entire game (innocuously, courtesy of a double play), and Terry's throwing a shutout and is still in there. Seth is struck by how baseball has changed in the pitching department over the past five decades. He is thinking about how back then, in the fifties and sixties, men were men and the game, like this game he's observing, was dominated by the very human being who initiates the action.

About how the major leagues' leading pitchers of that era, men of toughness and stamina and hurling gravitas, read like a Hall of Fame roll call: Raschi, Reynolds, Lopat, Ford, Lemon, Feller, Wynn, Garcia, Pierce, Trucks, Shantz,

Garver, Ramos, Pascual, Bunning, Kaat, McLain, Lolich, Hunter, Lonborg, Chance, Palmer, McNally, Cuellar, and then Roberts, Simmons, Black, Newcombe, Roe, Labine, Erskine, Loes, Podres, Drysdale, Koufax, Maglie, Jansen, Hearn, Antonelli, Gomez, Marichal, Spahn, Sain, Burdette, Blackwell, Dickson, Haddix, Friend, Nuxhall, Gibson, Bunning, Perry, Jenkins, Seaver . . . About how today's specialist firefighters, the relief pitchers who come in for an inning or even an out and make multimillions to do so, have altered the game, by transmogrifying those wonderful, old-fashioned, blue-collar, bite-your-lip-and-hang-in-there-till-the-bitter-end starters into dinosaurs.

The pride of going the distance and toughing it out is an aspect of the game Seth really misses. Hearing about guys like old Warren Spahn, a workhorse who had twenty or more complete games in twelve different seasons, 382 in his career.

Three hundred eighty-two!

He recalls Papa Sol's recounting to him once or twice that incredible game of May 26, 1959, when the Pirates' Harvey Haddix pitched twelve perfect innings against the Milwaukee Braves, only to lose it in the thirteenth on the Braves' only hit, a homer (technically ruled a double) by Joe Adcock. And the Kitten was beaten by Lew Burdette, who himself pitched a complete game! The two starters totaled an inconceivable twenty-five and two-thirds innings pitched, only one walk, and zero earned runs.

You start something, you finish it, Papa Sol used to say.

His grandfather also used to regale him with the story of the heroic pitching duel between Juan Marichal and Warren Spahn on July 2, 1963, right here at the 'Stick, in which each pitcher toiled for fifteen scoreless innings . . . *apiece!* When the Say Hey Kid hit a dinger off Spahnie in the bottom of the sixteenth, each hurler had thrown over two hundred pitches. Sol enjoyed comparing both pitching warriors to the heroes of Greek mythology who toiled in battle against monsters: Bellerophon, Hercules, Perseus, Theseus.

"Are the Giants gonna score now, Dad?" Simon inquires.

"I hope so, Simaroo. This is their last chance, but, yeah, I think we're due, you just watch. In fact, I give you my word they'll score two now and win the game."

"Yay! And beat the damn Yankees?"

Papa Sol nods.

It is indeed the Giants' last chance and here's Matty Alou pinch-hitting for reliever Billy O'Dell and Sol and Simon are both crossing their fingers like mad and Seth isn't because he already knows the outcome and reliable Matty beats out a gorgeous drag bunt just to the right of the mound. (It is 1962, Seth notes, well before the bunt became extinct.)

It's only the third hit off Terry, who's been pitching a masterpiece. Simon draws over the line from home to first on the little diamond in his scorecard. Papa Sol smiles approvingly and pats his son on the top of the head.

Sol points out the base path between first and second, tells Simon about how they named it "Maury's Lake," because when the Giants played the Dodgers and their premium base stealer Maury Wills, the grounds crew would drench the dirt there so he couldn't run as fast.

So there stands Matty Alou at first and up comes his big brother, Felipe. Like Newk in the '51 pennant game, Terry is on the hill throwing smoke, gas, heaters, darts, bullets, pills, pellets, aspirin tablets, cheese, the old Pepper, plus he's pulling the string and making ol' Uncle Charlie drop off the table, so even the solid Felipe doesn't stand a chance and whiffs.

Simon pouts and writes a *K* in the middle of the score-card diamond.

And here comes weak-hitting Chuck Hiller. Terry delivers an aspirin tablet and the attendees at Candlestick expel a collective *oooooh* as dirt that has been lying caked and fallow inside Ellie Howard's catcher's mitt explodes in all directions when the ball makes impact, like dust shooting out of a Persian rug that has just been spanked by a batwing beater. Howard winces and fires the ball back to Terry and Papa Sol is getting mighty nervous. And before you know it, Hiller is down on strikes, too, and Seth's dad sadly writes in another *K* and now there are two gone and the Giants are down to their final out in this deciding game of the 1962 World Series.

But hope springs eternal for Giants fans, who still remember what happened with Bobby Thomson against Ralph Branca when all seemed lost eleven years ago.

Papa Sol looks at the scorecard and licks his chops, knowing full well that his hero, Willie Mays, will be coming up, with the menacing McCovey on deck and the dangerous Cepeda in the hole.

"Just you watch, Simaroo. These next three guys may be the most powerful hitting tandem in baseball history, maybe even more explosive than the Yankees' 1927 Murderers' Row of Ruth, Gehrig, Meusel, and Lazzeri."

Simon licks his chops, too.

"Now batting for the Giants, number twenty-four, the center fielder, Willie Mays," the PA announcer bellows.

Bedlam.

Seth sees the hope flicker in his grandfather's eyes as the announcement is made, because the game now rests

upon the shoulders of the hero of Papa Sol and, by hered-
ity, of Simon and Seth, too. With one stroke of Willie's bat,
one flick of his powerful wrists, the game will be History.

Willie!

Willie, Mickey, and the Duke? *Fuhgeddaboudit!* Tallu-
lah Bankhead was right: "There have been only two ge-
niuses in the world. Willie Mays and Willie Shakespeare."
And like his Elizabethan predecessor, Willie could sure
make plays.

Willie!

A real artist up there, innovative, thrilling to watch, inimit-
able. After he was born, the mold became smithereens. Has
a sixth sense and a flair for drama, whether it is baserun-
ning, his unique basket catch, sliding and losing his cap,
making unforgettable catches and throws, getting a quick
jump on a fly ball, or producing runs at the critical juncture
of a game.

Willie!

This year alone, the producer of forty-nine homers and
141 ribbies. And the one guy in the solar system you'd want
up there swinging for the fences with the tilt on the line.

Willie!

Six hundred sixty career dingers when he finally retired
as a Met, and one right here and right now would be just
what the carpenter ordered.

Willie!

Sensing blood, Sol's nostrils twitch in the chill mid-October air. Seth watches his grandfather and imagines him
and his finely tuned baseball mind thinking things through,
like an international chess grandmaster anticipating the next
three moves.

"Now just watch ol' Willie do his thing, Simaroo. If
anyone can come through, he's your man."

Right on cue, Willie doesn't disappoint. He grips his bat with that trademark right thumb pointing straight up to the heavens and does that familiar hip wiggle and takes that wide stance and digs in at the plate.

Smack!

Terry's heater is rifled down the right-field line, ball exiting batter's box even more rapidly than when it entered. Alou glides into third, Mays chugs around to second, but what goes unnoticed, perhaps to all but historian Seth, is what Roger Maris is doing out there in the right-field corner, which is nothing short of saving the game and the Series. He is playing the carom perfectly and throwing a strike to cutoff man Richardson and holding Alou, the potential tying run, at third.

Oh, breaking* the Babe's unbreakable* thirty-four-year-old home-run record* was nice, Seth thinks, but this unheralded, unassuming defensive play might well have been Roger's crowning baseball achievement.

Second and third, and the Jints are either one out away from losing the Series or one hit away from winning it. And, second move on the chessboard, McCovey and Cepeda are due up.

Historian Seth realizes that men were also on second and third as a result of a single and a double when Thomson stepped to the plate against Branca.

The tension is palpable and Papa Sol and his teenage son have their four eyes glued to the action and the winds are now gusting up to thirty knots, coming in from dead center, and Seth Stein is wondering why he has been brought here, to this particular game at this particular moment.

Terry rubs the ball in his hands and knows he is going to have an unwelcome visitor. Sure enough, here's Yankees manager Ralph Houk exiting the dugout and beginning his trek to the mound to lecture his tiring pitcher.

As Houk's head emerges, Solomon Stein puts his carpenter's right hand on the figurative chesspiece and makes his move. He is barely ten feet away from the Yankees manager now, and his yowl sure gets the skipper's attention.

"Hey, Ralph, remember Maz? *Take the bum out!*"

Seth catches on to his grandfather's creative chess gambit: The savvy Sol is employing reverse psychology here, knowing full well that a mere two years ago, Terry, in an eerily similar situation, gave up that winning homer to Mazeroski. Sol knows how nervous Terry must be with the deciding Series game on the line once again and is counting on manager Houk to bristle at a Giants fan telling him to yank Terry out of the game and, out of stubbornness, to do exactly the opposite and leave his nervous, tiring pitcher in.

It is a managerial decision for the ages, a move that reflects the beauty and complexity of baseball strategy and decision making. Maybe Houk is thinking about Chuck Dressen's taking Newk out for Branca in '51, and you know what happened then. Which is exactly what does not happen now: Bill Stafford, who won the third game, and Bud Daley are warming up in the bull pen, but, egged on by Sol's taunt, Houk has already decided to leave Terry in the game as he approaches the mound.

"All right, now listen up, you sonuvabitch," Houk fumes. "Can you get this one friggin' guy out? *Look me in the eyes when I'm talking to you, goddammit!*"

Terry obeys and stares at his manager with eyes that cannot conceal the fear.

"Yes, sir. I got this guy in my hip pocket."

"You sonuvabitch. Now don't you go thinking about this guy's triple in the seventh. And don't you go thinking about what happened a few years ago."

Houk is using tough love and his decades of baseball experience to goad his pitcher into focusing on the present and performing at an exceedingly high level, but in point of fact Ralph Terry feels like puking right about now.

Manager pats pitcher on the tush and lumbers back to the dugout.

Back to the chessboard. In his seat, arm around his son, a self-satisfied Sol knows that his move has succeeded brilliantly and that, what's more, now that Houk is leaving Terry in, he has undoubtedly instructed him to pitch to McCovey, because of Cepeda's statistical edge this season (Stretch only played in ninety-one games, but no matter). Hits: 191–67, 2B: 26–6, HR: 35–20, RBI: 114–54, BA: .306–.293, HBP: 6–0. Plus, even though Terry hadn't walked a batter, putting McCovey on would load the bases and create an intolerably precarious situation. Plus, McCovey is a rookie. But this is exactly what Papa Sol wants. He's got the righty/lefty matchup. And in Game 2, McCovey had homered late in the game (in the seventh), hadn't he?, off a similarly tiring Terry (just like Bobby Thomson had homered off a tiring Branca in Game 1 before the Big One two games later). And don't forget that in this game, he'd also hit that triple in the seventh.

Solomon Stein likes the odds. And to think it was his resourceful taunt that set up this whole hopeful scenario.

"C'mon, Willie, just a little bingle, that's all we need!" a rejuvenated Sol shouts.

"C'mon, Willie, a little bingle!" Simon Stein parrots.

The imposing six-feet-four McCovey steps up to the plate and waves his bat menacingly behind him. In his huge hands, it looks like the proverbial toothpick. He takes the first pitch for a ball. Sol and Simon and Seth Stein and the other 43,946 spectators are at the edge of their seats.

On the second offering, the rookie absolutely torches one that curves just foul down the right-field line. Hearts are in throats at the near miss, and, unnoticed, this rope of a line drive has prompted second sacker Bobby Richardson to move three baby steps to his left and toward first base.

On the third pitch, Stretch is jammed but somehow, miraculously, adjusts in mid-swing and scorches another liner that looks for all the world like it is heading over Richardson's head and safely into right field for the game winner. But the ball is sinking with topspin, and Bobby, who had just repositioned himself, moves slightly to his left and reaching but without leaping barely nabs the shot for the final, excruciating out.

Papa Sol is aghast. His "Take the bum out!" strategy—so masterful, so well conceived—has backfired. And his Jints have let him down. And he has let his Simaroo down.

Simon, sensing his dad's despondency even at his formative age, puts his arm around his father's shoulder.

"It's only a game, Pop," Simon consoles, with wisdom beyond his years.

◖◗

"It's only a game," Seth consoles, standing behind his Papa Sol in the living room in Berkeley as his grandfather, alone in the house this morning, reads the front page of the *San Francisco Chronicle*.

"Take the bum out!" a forlorn Sol whispers to himself as he looks at the photo of Bobby Richardson nabbing McCovey's rope.

"Take the bum out!"

Papa Sol tilts his head back and looks straight up, as if his empty stare could shoot through the ceiling and the roof and go directly to the Almighty to seek comfort.

His eyes are piercing straight through Seth's invisible eyes.

Seth sees the same odd look on Sol's face as when he was scrutinizing the clipping in his Brooklyn basement, the article about the hundreds of fans claiming they had the "authentic" Bobby Thomson ball. A shiver of fear courses through Seth's body.

Papa Sol's look is searing into Seth's brain, etching itself indelibly. It is almost too painful to return the look.

Seth closes his eyes.

⚾

Seth opens his eyes. To his left is his Martin 000-28EC, just where he had left it, resting on its little stand in his Cambridge study. Straight ahead, on the coffee table, is the scuffed baseball reposing in its custom-made, green-felt niche. The wooden box's hinged top is open. He is slumped in his La-Z-Boy. His watch says it is 12:15 A.M.

This is getting too strange, Seth thinks, closing the top of the wooden box and reflecting on his second trip to the past.

He is thinking about how he has witnessed a second huge disappointment in the life of baseball fanatic Solomon Stein, a second scenario in which his grandfather's high baseball hopes have tumbled down to earth. First the worthless Thomson baseball, now the Terry Fiasco. Is this turning into a dangerous pattern in Papa Sol's secret life? Are these two baseball games he has revisited with his grandfather simply games, or mirrors of some deeper conflict in Sol's psyche that no one ever knew about? Was Sol somehow crazy enough about the game and his team to . . . take his own life?

He is thinking about how this exciting game was one of the most vivid reflections of how baseball is a game of inches, about how McCovey's drive might have sailed above Richardson's head and into the outfield if it were just a few inches higher, or if Richardson hadn't repositioned himself those few inches toward first base, thus making the Giants and not the hated Yanks World Champions, about how this game is such a powerful metaphor for life. He is thinking about all the near misses that have occurred not only in baseball, but in History, and in his own thirty-three years, and about how much of life is out of one's control and often depends on a lucky bounce or a chance encounter or a twist of fate.

He is thinking, too, about all the times that Papa Sol, and Seth Stein, and everyone on the face of the earth now and in History and for all time to come have ever taken three baby steps to the left—or not—and about how that has made all the difference.

An exhausted Seth considers crashing for the night, but he's got too much work, between tinkering with the book and preparing for tomorrow's class.

He picks up the phone, and his fingers dial a number they know by rote.

"Kate? It's Seth. I *know* it's late. I'm sorry, sweetie. But we have to talk. . . . How 'bout tomorrow, after squash, at noon? Great. Love you, too."

4

CURSE

THE FIGURE IN THE MIRROR looking outward at its source resembles an untoasted marshmallow more than it does Seth Stein.

Before he quaffs his morning joe, Seth possesses the approximate vision of a newborn sea otter. Which explains why he can't see much of anything as he lathers up his face with shaving cream.

His implements of depilation: Merkur double-edge safety razor, Kent silver-tip badger shaving brush with white hand-turned barrel, Solomon Stein Honduran mahogany shaving bowl with sandalwood soap. All presented to him by Papa Sol on the occasion of his very first shave seventeen years ago.

His entire face south of his eyes is under lather. A horizontal wipe of the index finger across the lips creates a window in the middle of the foamy mass, not so much for aesthetic purposes as for the fact that he now has the option of breathing through his mouth if he so desires.

As he strokes his cheek with the blade, his mouth forming a capital *O*, the marshmallow in the mirror becomes a face, which Seth recognizes as his own—yes, those are his piercing brown eyes, and there's the strong nose Papa Sol bequeathed to him, and the full head of jet-black hair, too. Yup, it is for certain the face of Seth Stein, Seth notes as he approaches wakefulness.

He is nearly three-quarters of the way through his shaving ritual, his vision is about 80 percent, and he is acclimating to his bathroom surroundings.

When suddenly his hand, the one holding the razor, stops dead in its tracks, halfway down his left cheek.

Seth squints, refocuses, parks his razor on the side of the sink, opens his eyes extra wide to get the clearest possible corroborating view.

His vision restored, he is staring at a wicked sunburn that begins at the top of his forehead, continues down his face and neck, and ends in a *V* halfway between his clavicles and his sternum. Which is odd, because it's mid-October in Cambridge, the temps are in the forties, and the sun has been on sabbatical for weeks.

Holy kamoley.

◖C◗

A clean-shaven Seth is sitting alone at a table in the Algiers Coffee House, on Brattle Street, waiting to be joined by his best friend, Gordon Stewart. He slowly sips his Arabic coffee, the best you can find outside of Abu Dhabi. *Ahhh.*

The coffee-*cum*-stimulating conversation with Gordon is a lovely daily morning ritual, usually followed by a drive to the squash courts at the Murr Center on North Harvard Street on the other side of the Charles River, then a hotly contested match that often goes the full five games, and a hot shower. Today is particularly hectic for Seth: From the shower, he will have that talk with Kate, grab a quick lunch, teach his two o'clock class with the bushy-tailed freshmen, spend a couple of hours working on his book in his Robinson Hall office, have a phone chat with Sammy, pay a sweet visit to Elsie, and top it all off with a relaxing, romantic dinner and evening with Kate.

Here comes ol' Gordon, with the usual swagger in his step. He is thirty-four, witty, ebullient, erudite, charming, African American. Husband of Kate's best friend, Molly. Amazing athlete. Successful shrink with a booming practice.

"Buon giorno, èbete!" Gordon booms.

"Shalom! Achotcha zona!" Seth shouts.

"Mon cul, espèce de crétin!"

"Guten Morgen, Scheißkopf!"

"You are *cracked!*"

"Why, *ibid.,* I'm sure!"

"*Loc. cit.!*"

"You should be *locked* up!"

"*Sic passim!*"

"You are one *sick* puppy!"

"*Et al.!*"

"You can call me *Al!*"

"Hey, *Al!*"

The lightning exchange epitomizes the friendship, with its Marx Brothers zaniness, Henny Youngman pacing, Jerry Lewis intonation, Monty Python erudition. When they are together, Seth and Gordon are certifiably out of their respective gourds.

Gordon purchases his cup of java, joins Seth at the table. Seeing Seth's sunburn, he does a double take.

"So whassup, my bro?" Gordon asks his darker-skinned-than-usual friend.

"Same old. Book's proceeding apace. Teaching's fun. Kate's great—"

"Hubba hubba—"

"Moron!"

"So, what do the Sox have to do to win the pennant again?" Gordon inquires, taking a first sip of his Arabic.

"Yeah, damn Yankees," Seth says. "Well, here's my theory. The pitching is about even, and we can't trade for another Pedro or Clemens, because we'd have to unload damn near half the team to get them. So I say we win it with *fighters*. Fill our lineup with feisty, gritty, scrappy, gutsy guys. Guys who never give up. Get Bill Mueller and Johnny Damon back, trade for David Eckstein, bring Wally Backman and Pete Rose and Lenny Dykstra out of retirement, resurrect Richie Ashburn, and we'll have Ortiz and Ramirez and seven table-setters in the lineup and hope the pitching holds up."

"Y'know, I think you're on to something here. Very creative. Me, I've always believed that old saw that good pitching will always beat good hitting. So I'd trade for Johan Santana, John Smoltz, Jake Peavy, and Mariano Rivera . . . and *screw* the lineup!"

"Great minds think differently," Seth says between sips.

"So, anything happening outside the box?" Gordon says.

"Well, now that you ask, yeah. But you'll never believe me."

"Shoot."

"Gordon?" Seth chooses his words with great care. "Lately, well, I've been seeing . . . Papa Sol."

"How do you mean? And remember, the meter's running."

"Hardy-har-har. No, seriously, I saw him twice, and it was *amazing.*"

A hesitant Seth is torn between spilling his guts to Gordon, telling him everything just the way it happened or at least the way he thought it happened, and zipping his lip until he knows the whole story.

"I don't know if they were dreams or not," he fudges. "I think they were, but they seemed so goddam *real.*"

Gordon affects a thick, mock–Sigmund Freud accent. "Well, then, let us see. Very interesting case. You say you are dreaming you saw your Papa Sol, yes?"

"Gor-don!"

"Yes, it is obvious," Gordon continues, his Austrian accent thickening, "that since the dream is the royal road to the unconscious, your dreams of Papa Sol are disguises for wish fulfillment, the wish to see him again, yes, and to satisfy your repressed feelings of abandonment and resentment."

"Are you quite finished?" Seth asks.

"Not quite," Gordon answers, thickening his accent even more. "From a Jungian perspective, I would even say that these dreams are a compensation for, a reaction to, your traumatic experience in real life, allowing you free access to the collective unconscious and its primordial archetypes, where your seeing your grandfather represents, symbolically, the archetypal motifs of the Shadow, the Persona, the Anima, the Trickster, and the Puer Aeternus, all at the same time."

Gordon is milking it for all it's worth but, seeing by the look on Seth's tightened face that he has gone too far, ends his little jocular therapy session.

"I'm sorry, but your time is up," Gordon announces

lamely. "Seriously, Seth, tell me about it, really. I'm all ears."

Seth weighs his options. He wants to speak candidly to Gordon, get his professional and personal take on things. But as close as Gordon is to him, how could he possibly believe what Seth is about to tell him? Believe that he actually saw Sol in the flesh as he was back then? Believe that he was there with Sol at the Polo Grounds and Candlestick? What a Freudian field day he'd have should Seth inform him about checking in on his three-year-old father. And what about the ticket stub and the mustard stain and the sunburn as prima facie evidence? Would Gordon actually believe him or call for the men in the white jackets to haul him away to the funny farm?

Seth gets a chill thinking that he is very possibly experiencing the same fear that Papa Sol must have felt, the fear that no one would believe his stories, of the Catch and the Ball and the Taunt, and would simply dismiss them as being absurd.

"Gordon, I'm telling you, it all seemed so *real . . . ,*" Seth begins but can't pull the trigger.

"I'll bet. It's pretty normal, actually, your wanting to reconnect with him, sort things out, come to a resolution, reconfirm your love—"

"Yeah, I guess. It was great. And I saw sides to Papa Sol I never knew about."

"This is normal, too. You're probably compensating for your loss of him by building him up, dimensionalizing your image of him to accentuate the positive."

"But, Gordon, I'm not sure why I'm dreaming about him now, or why—"

"We never know why we dream what we dream or why we do it when we do it," Gordon consoles his best friend.

"Listen, kiddo, this is all perfectly normal and understandable. You're still recovering from what happened, it seems to me, and your wounds are still healing, even after all this time. It's just natural you'd want to be with him again, it's as simple as that. Well, not really, but that's the nub of it."

"Hey, thanks for listening to all this silliness," Seth says.

"No problemo, my bro," Gordon says, with a wink. "Just send me a check."

⚾

Seth rings the buzzer, and Kate answers it, looking her perky, adorable self.

"Hey, babe," she says, planting a warm kiss on his lips. "Whassup?"

"I just . . . wanted to tell you how much I love you."

"That's *it*?" Kate says, leading Seth to the sofa. "I mean, that's wonderful, but . . . I thought you had something pressing to tell me, by the sound of your voice on the phone last night."

"That *is* something pressing. I'm sorry I woke you up, and I'm sorry I might have worried you, but I wanted you to know."

"I know you love me," a disappointed Kate says, "but . . . I guess I thought you were talking about *another* pressing matter." Kate gives Seth *that* look, and Seth gets it.

It's time to talk turkey, but he's feeling a little chicken.

"Oh, that? Well, my dearest, you know how much I love you, and I've given it some serious thought, really I have. I've just been waiting for the right time. But, well, I'm not sure if that time is now."

"But why not now, sweetie? I think now's a perfectly perfect time."

"Kate, it's just that . . . well, if you must know, I still

have that awful taste in my mouth from my divorce from Julie, even now. I can't seem to get that out my head. I know it doesn't make sense, but there it is. And aside from all my work, the teaching and the meetings and the book I'm struggling with, I still have to spend part of my time raising Sammy—"

"But—"

"And then there's the issue of my heart disease. The by-pass surgery is still with me, not physically, but in the way I feel deep inside every single day, and love you as I do, I just don't ever want to make you feel pain or . . . make you . . . a widow. . . ."

Kate blinks her eyes and sets her jaw. "I know, my sweetie, I know, but I do love you so much, and none of that matters, not if we love each other as much as we do."

Seth looks at Kate, and then into his soul. On top of everything else, he wonders, what if she doesn't believe me when I do tell her about Papa Sol and my visits to the past? What if we plan a wedding and a life together, and then she ends up not trusting me and calling the asylum to have her lunatic hubby put away?

"Honey," Kate implores, "I just think it's time we made a commitment to each other—"

"I know that's how you feel, Kate . . . but, well, let me put it another way."

Seth searches for the right words.

"Do you remember my telling you about that famous playoff game between the Giants and Dodgers in '51? The one where Bobby Thomson hit that dramatic ninth-inning homer off Ralph Branca?"

Kate nods of course she does but wonders where this is going.

"Well, during his at bat against Branca, Bobby sees two

pitches. On the first one, he isn't committed, because of the fears he has standing there at the plate. He's as nervous as a kitten and just isn't ready to be in the batter's box at that moment and to commit to his pitch, with all that pressure and all those things flying around in his brain. So he stands there like a statue, the bat frozen on his shoulder, and watches a strike blow right by him."

Kate starts to catch on.

"And so, my sweetheart, it isn't until the second pitch that he becomes more relaxed, and by then the time is right, and he's prepared to swing and commit totally to it, and the rest is History."

Kate gets it.

Seth leaves it at that. He loves the fact that although she doesn't really follow baseball, she does respect his passion for the game and tries hard to understand its intricacies and life lessons. Unlike a certain ex.

Part of Kate wants to rant and yell and scream about the fact that she's worked her butt off to get to where she is professionally and now she is finally free to devote some quality time and her heart and her soul to the man she so desperately loves and then what about the issue of her biological clock ticking now that she's turned thirty and sometimes it is ticking so loud she can't get it out of her head, just like Captain Hook obsessing about that clock that his nemesis the crocodile had swallowed.

Kate's eyes are moist, and so are Seth's. The four eyes are moist with a little sadness and frustration, but mostly with love and caring.

"I love you, Seth Stein."

"I love you, Kate Richman."

Seth is sitting in his kitchen, thinking about the morning coffee chat with Gordon and the brief encounter at noon with Kate. About how he didn't have the guts to tell his best friend what really happened with Papa Sol, in exquisite detail. About how he didn't have the nerve to tell Kate, either. What a wuss.

No, he *isn't* a wuss. He just thought that neither would believe him, not really, that they'd think he was cracked or at the very least a touch unstable. Or was it that he still needed more conclusive proof that what happened wasn't a dream or a hallucination?

But it's a gorgeous, crisp Cambridge autumn Saturday morning and Kate is at her place, working on new recipes for seafood stew (*ciotola di mare*) and terra-cotta chicken (*pollo nel coccio*), and Seth is luxuriating in the very thought of a once-in-a-blue-moon Solo Breakfast Special and it's time to get crackin'.

Seth whirls into action. He is performing his special Gene Kelly morning choreography, straight from the opening scene of *An American in Paris*. With precise, athletic movements that are at once frenetic and graceful, he flicks on a light, opens a pantry door, removes a box of matzoh, kicks the door closed, greases the pan, grinds the beans, pours the water, opens the fridge door, removes the eggs, kicks the door closed, scrambles the eggs, crumbles the matzoh, soaks and drains it, adds and mixes the eggs plus onion powder, heats the pan, opens the fridge, removes the oranges, kicks the door closed, squeezes the oranges, fries the matzoh-egg mix, pours the juice, opens the fridge, takes out the fruit, kicks the door closed, tears off a paper towel, opens the drawer, removes a fork and a spoon, knees the drawer closed, spoons out the fruit, serves the matzoh, pours the coffee, proceeds *à table*.

He performs these terpsichorean feats in rapid succession, with a multitasking suppleness of all his extremities that would make an octopus turn green.

Spread before Seth on the kitchen table is a breakfast that would make even the most jaded food critic *plotz*. Including: a tall glass of freshly squeezed OJ; a piping hot cup of Peet's Indonesian Garuda Blend coffee, served black; a plate of Papa Sol's special pancake-style matzoh brie, with salt sprinkled on top; and for dessert, a bowl of Fresh Fruit Gingerbubbly, a yummy concoction he'd learned from his Tar Heel friends, Beth and Jake Billwith, which consists of champagne, sugar, and fresh, peeled ginger, strained and poured over sliced oranges, strawberries, kiwi, melon, and pineapple (all of which has been blissfully fermenting overnight in the fridge).

In a little under nine minutes, Seth finishes the regal breakfast, and as he polishes off the last morsel of Korbel-soaked kiwi, he has an epiphany.

Of course. Papa Sol would never have used a capital *A* in the word *Attic* in his note by chance, nor would he have made a careless error. No, he was a meticulous man, from his exquisite carpentry to his obsessive love of linguistic niceties to virtually everything he did and said. So he couldn't have meant that he left something for Seth in the attic of his house as a legacy. The only other meaning that occurs to Seth, then, is that Sol's legacy to him has to do with something Greek.

But what?

For now, all he can think of is the world of Greek mythology that Papa Sol had taught him so well and so caringly, something to do with that? A lesson in one or more of the myths, perhaps? Or maybe he left him a special, brand-new book of Greek mythology somewhere?

From his perch in culinary heaven, Seth is brought down to earth with this line of thinking. He's got Papa Sols on the brain now. Papa Sol the loving, giving grandfather reading stories to him. Papa Sol the private, passionate man at the ballparks and reading the newspaper articles. Papa Sol the tormented soul with an S&W .38 pressed against his temple. The Papa Sol whose secrets he can't yet divulge even to his loved ones. The Papa Sol who, goddammit, still owes him answers.

Seth walks to Papa Sol's wooden box in the study. He's been avoiding it lately. Hasn't had the time for it. Has been digesting his visits to the past, debating whether to share them. Is maybe a tiny bit nervous about what else he'll discover.

Seth is ready now. He opens the top of the box, grabs the ball and grips it in his right hand. Even squeezes it, as if to implore it to yield more answers, to take him back one more time and let him at last get to the bottom of it all.

Sweet Momma.

Room spins, faster, Oz music—*Dah-de-lah-de-lah*—feeling of calm, Beatles' riff, Slide Show.

What and who'll it be *this* time? *Aha.*

The invention of the sundial and the founding of Carthage and Nero fiddles and the Norman Conquest and the Crusades and Marie Antoinette at the guillotine and the Bill of Rights and the Louisiana Purchase and Darwin publishes *The Origin of Species* and the stock market crash and astronauts land on the moon and Nixon's presidency implodes and the Challenger explodes . . .

And the final burst of the Beatles' riff and the rousing, raucous, brash, clashing, strident, high-pitched, piercing, trumpety climax. And the tornado grinds to a halt. And

Seth is deposited gently on the ground. It is no longer 2006.

Ⓒ

It is 1986.

Seth knows it is, because he is standing in a very familiar kitchen, Papa Sol and Grandma Elsie's in Cambridge, and on the table is a copy of *Time* magazine with Reagan and Gorbachev on the cover under the type:

TIME
NO DEAL
Star Wars Sinks the Summit

Over the red *E* of TIME: $1.95. Over the *T*: OCTOBER 20, 1986.

Seth compares the kitchen with the ones he visited in 1951 and 1962. The stooping, slouching cavemen of kitchens past have evolved into one who is fully erect, with all the modern gadgets you could ask for: spiffy three-door fridge with through-the-door ice and water service, electric stove, microwave oven, toaster oven, digital clock radio, Cuisinart.

The kitchen is, of course, spotless.

Seth is used to visiting the past by now, but he still finds it strange to be in Sol and Elsie's house back then. He hears Papa Sol's familiar voice and bounds up the thirteen creaky stairs to investigate.

The voice is coming from the second bedroom.

Didn't that used to be *my* room?

Reaching the threshold, Seth looks into a bedroom filled with dusk. He is standing behind Papa Sol, who is sitting on the bed of a prepubescent boy. The boy's deep brown eyes sparkle and widen, peeking over the covers, Kilroy-like, as his grandpa's deep, mellifluent voice speaks to him, his majestic baritone meticulously caressing each syllable. The boy looks uncannily like Seth Stein.

The boy *is* Seth Stein.

Papa Sol is now fifty-eight. A reasonable amount of salt has been shaken on the pepper in his hair and beard, and a few rogue wrinkles furrow his brow. On his lap is a copy of the sports section of the *Boston Globe* of Friday, October 24, 1986, its headline gloating about the Bosox victory over the Mets, 4–2, in Game 5 of the World Series, to take a 3–2 lead in games.

"And now for your very special bedtime story, Setharoo," Papa Sol announces.

The entranced thirteen-year-old waits breathlessly. He adores his bedtime baseball stories, even at his ripe old age.

"It's called 'The Curse.' *Wooooooooo!*" Sol sings scarily in a trilly, ghostlike, gradually descending soprano.

The younger of the two Seths in the room shivers in mock fear from underneath the covers.

"Are you quite ready for me to continue, young whipper-snapper?" Papa Sol asks.

Younger Seth nods.

Older Seth thinks it's pretty freaky watching the earlier version of himself being read to by Papa Sol. But he remembers the story and feels the love and wipes a misty eye.

"Okay then, heeeeere we go! 'The Curse,' by Papa Solomon Stein. Once upon a time, and a very long time ago it was, there lived a mighty baseball team. And the name of this team was . . . the *Bosox!*"

Younger Seth giggles.

"Well, this team was as mighty as mighty could be. Yes

indeedy," Sol intones, affecting a pronounced W. C. Fields voice to spice up the action. "Had players the likes of Cy Young and Tris Speaker, yeeesss."

Younger Seth is in stitch.

"Not to mention, lemme see, oh yeeesss, Eddie Cicotte and Gavvy Cravath and Dutch Leonard and Ernie Shore and Heinie Wagner and Tricky Chickie Shorten."

And now in stitches.

"And Waite Hoyt and Bullet Joe Bush and Sad Sam Jones and Herbie Pennock, yesssss, and Jack Stuffy McInnis and Everett Deacon Scott and Harry Hoop Hooper and Braggo Globetrotter Roth."

And now completely beside himself.

"And another feller you mighta heard of, a feller named George Herman Ruth, *the Babe*," Papa Sol whispers importantly. The bedroom turns silent.

"Well, my little man, these mighty Bosox teams, they were the scourge of the country back then, yessirreeeee. Played in five World Series, and y'know how many of 'em they won?"

Younger Seth looks adoringly at Papa Sol, shakes his head. Older Seth, in possession of the correct answer, blurts to a deaf audience, *"Five!"*

"Five!" Sol answers. "Yessirree Bob, five outta five. Whatta team!"

Papa Sol trades in his jocular Fields voice for Vincent Price's scary and sinister baritone.

"And then, just before the baseball season of nineteen hundred and twenty, do you know what happened, my boy?"

"N-n-no." If younger Seth were wearing boots, he'd be shaking in them.

Papa Sol scrunches up his eyes, moves his face to

within two inches of younger Seth's, and, in a deep voice that quakes and is filled with evil and foreboding, enunciates the two most harrowing syllables younger Seth has ever heard.

"The *Curse!*"

Gasp. Shudder.

"Yes, it was the *Curse* that happened to these brave and mighty Bosox boys, just as sure as I'm sitting here telling you this terrible tale. The *Curse* befell them, a *Curse* so powerful and insidious that no one who donned a Bosox uniform was brave or mighty or strong enough to lift it."

Papa Sol stops, overcome by mock exhaustion, takes a breather.

Younger Seth is hanging on every syllable, wrapped up hook, line, and sinker in the action. Older Seth is, too.

"Where was I?" Papa Sol asks. "Ah yes," he continues in his evil and foreboding baritone. "It was the *Curse,* I tell you, the *Curse* . . . of the Bam**BI**no!" he exclaims, pronouncing the last word in a poetic Tuscan dialect worthy of Dante Alighieri, with the exquisitely enunciated accent falling squarely on the middle syllable.

"This, my young man, was the greatest *Curse* of all time, greater than the *Curse* of Sleeping Beauty, greater even than the *Curse* of the House of Atreus. Yes, this *Curse* was . . ."

A hush.

". . . the *Curse* . . . of the Bam**BI**no!"

"*Ooooooooh!*" the two Seths whisper simultaneously.

"Aye, mark me words, laddie," Papa Sol says, switching seamlessly to his Long John Silver voice. "This was not just yer normal, everyday curse, a curse that might last a day er a week er a month er even a year. This was not a curse that would pass before too long a time, that would just go *poof!* one fine day and be over with. *Nae!* And d'you know *why?*"

Again, silence.

"Because it was—*aaargh!*—the *Curse* . . . of the Bam-**BI**no!

"Aye, it all happened on that fateful day of January the third, nineteen hundred and twenty—remember the date well, me laddie—when a certain Mister Harry Frazee committed the dastardly deed of selling the great Babe Ruth, the mightiest of the mighty Bosox—the Bam**BI**no!—for one hundred and twenty-five thousand smackeroos, just to save his wretched hide and pay the rent! Shipped Babe off—*aaargh!*—like a head of cattle, like a miserable slave, Harry did, and d'you know what was the worst thing of all about this dastardly deed?"

"N-n-no," the two Seths answer concurrently.

"He shipped the great and mighty Bam**BI**no off to . . . *the hated Yankees!*

"*Woooooooooo!*" Sol sings scarily in a trilly, ghostlike, gradually descending soprano.

Younger Seth hides his head under the covers, then reappears, a willing and eager sucker for more spooky stuff.

"Well now, me boy, here is the scariest part of the story!"

Both Seths quiver.

"The *Curse* . . . of the Bam**BI**no has lasted until this very day I am speaking to you! A grand total of . . . *sixty-six years!* Aye, ever since the Bam**BI**no was shipped off ignominiously by Mister Harry Frazee to the hated Yankees, d'ya know what has happened?"

"N-n-no," the Seths answer in unison.

"Well, the Bosox have won exactly no World Series, nothing, nada, zippo, zilch, nihil . . . ZERO!

"And d'ya know how many World Series the hated Yankees, the same hated Yankees who had never won bupkes before they acquired Babe Ruth, have won since the dastardly trade of the Bam**BI**no?"

"N-n-no."

"A grand total of . . . TWENTY-TWO!

"*Wooooooooo!*" Sol sings scarily in a trilly, ghostlike, gradually descending soprano.

Papa Sol rests again in mock exhaustion.

The mouths of both Seths are agape from Fear and Trembling.

Papa Sol's voice becomes mellow and kindly. "But do you know what?" he says.

"What?" the two Seths ask, breaths bated.

"This story has a happy ending! Yes, like all curses, *this* one is about to end!"

"Yay!" the two Seths cheer.

"Aye, tomorrow—remember the date well, me laddie (back to Long John Silver)—tomorrow is the day when the *Curse* ends at last! When the Bosox, the once again mighty Bosox, finish off the Mets in Game 6 and capture their first World Series since nineteen hundred and eighteen, their first in sixty-eight years, aye, capture a prize that is rightfully theirs! And *that,* me laddie—*aaargh!*—will be the end of the *Curse* . . ."

". . . of the Bam**BI**no!" the two Seths scream together in a hosanna of joy.

Younger Seth smiles and claps his hands in appreciation. So does older Seth.

"Now close your eyes, my Setharoo, and get some

sleep. It's time to visit the Yami of Yawn. Close your eyes now, that's my good boy . . . sleep. . . ."

And younger Seth closes his eyes and goes to a place far away.

And older Seth does the same.

◖◗

Seth Stein opens his eyes.

For once, he is not surprised to be where he is, in light of Sol's bedtime story, passion for his newly adopted team, and propensity to attend important ball games.

Seth is once again sitting in the lap of History, sitting on the field level in foul territory, even with first base, at Shea Stadium, home of the New York Mets, in Flushing Meadows, Queens.

He scans the outfield, recognizes the steep, five-tiered grandstands; the *Newsday* sign in left; then, behind the fence in center, the famous upside-down Mets Magic Top Hat, out of which rises a red Big Apple whenever a Met hits a homer; and, in right-center, the gargantuan 175-foot-long, 86-foot-high scoreboard with the Bulova clock on top and the huge ad:

THIS BUD'S FOR YOU.

His eyes gravitate to the running score at the base of the scoreboard:

Red Sox	110 000 100
Mets	000 020 010

Yep, it's the top of the tenth inning of Game 6 of the 1986 World Series all right, Seth thinks, verifying the numbers in his computer mind and filling in the final two that are missing:

Red Sox	110 000 100 2
Mets	000 020 010 3

One of the greatest baseball games ever played, one of the grittiest comebacks under pressure ever staged, and here he is, right in the thick of things.

Seth's eyes pan from the scoreboard to himself, identifying the Mets players in between, one by one: Mookie Wilson 1, Lenny Dykstra 4, and Darryl Strawberry 18 in the outfield; Ray Knight 22, Kevin Elster 2, Wally Backman 6, and Keith Hernandez 17 around the horn; Gary Carter 8 behind the plate and Rick Aguilera 38 on the mound.

The outfielders are pegging to one another, Hernandez is throwing grounders to his infield colleagues, and Aguilera is taking his eight warm-up pitches. The Changeless Face of Baseball, Seth is thinking.

What he is *really* thinking about is the historical significance of this particular game in the context of the fateful year of 1986. What his historian's brain is thinking about is the fact that in this year, there were four cataclysmic catastrophes that occurred on the planet, four disasters that brought sadness and anguish to a great many people. The technological disaster of January 28, the explosion of the Space Shuttle Challenger seventy-three seconds into its flight that killed teacher Christa McAuliffe and six other crew members. The nuclear disaster of April 26, the explosion and meltdown at Chernobyl that killed fifty-six people, with another nine thousand expected to die from solid cancers. The natural disaster of August 21, the limnic eruption of carbon dioxide at Lake Nyos, Cameroon, that killed more than seventeen hundred people. And the baseball disaster of October 25, perhaps the most tragic of all the catastrophes—the squirting of a ball through Bill Buckner's legs that killed the hopes and dreams of the many millions of inhabitants of Red Sox Nation throughout the world.

Which is about to transpire in approximately twenty-eight minutes.

Seth makes a mental note of the differences between the Polo Grounds and Shea. The Giants' ballpark was old and quirky, with odd dimensions, whereas Shea is more modern, more classic, with less character. There is a lot less smoking going on here. Baseball caps have replaced fedoras. Many more women are in attendance.

Sadly, thirty-five years later, one thing hasn't changed: Although there are a lot more black players in the majors, there are still, here and now, only two starting players for the home team who are African American (Strawberry and Wilson). Come to think of it, he computes, only two, as well, for the visitors (Jim Rice and Dave Henderson).

A low-flying plane rumbles overhead on its way to La-Guardia Airport.

Seth gets around to looking at his more immediate surroundings, namely, who is sitting next to him. Sure enough, there's fifty-eight-year-old Papa Sol seated to his left.

"Come on, Hendu!" Sol yells, as Dave Henderson, a dangerous Bosox hitter, strides up to the plate. "Hit one outta here!"

Historian Seth knows that Papa Sol will have his fervent wish granted in about two minutes.

As Hendu takes his warm-up swings and Aguilera fidgets on the mound, Seth notices that Sol is sitting next to, and chatting with, a woman. Not just any woman, mind you, but an extremely attractive woman, a green-eyed, dark-haired beauty of a woman, in her late thirties probably. Shades of Ava Gardner.

Huh?

Did Papa Sol lie to Elsie and sneak off to this ball game? To see this crucial contest, but also to be with . . . *her?*

Solomon Stein takes a recent photo of Seth out of his wallet and shows it to stunning Ava.

"Janet, you should see him. He's so bright, so handsome. He gives us such *naches!*"

Janet?

Janet dabs a tear that has formed in the corner of her right eye.

Seth is speechless. Who is this woman? In fact, who *the hell* is this woman? A girlfriend of Papa Sol's? An old friend? She seems too young. An old friend of Seth's parents, perhaps? Someone Sol just met and befriended? No, she's too emotional for that. Why is she crying over Seth? Does she *know* him?

"Thanks for sharing that with me, Solomon. Makes me feel good. Much appreciated."

"Welcome. Hey, think your ol' Mets can pull this one out?"

"You better believe it. Just watch."

"Well, we'll see about that," Sol says, then, looking out, "Okay, Hendu, it's your time to poke one outta here!"

Seth is trying to recall if he ever heard the name *Janet* uttered in the Stein household. Nope.

Strike one to Hendu. Then, on an 0-1 count, *pow!* outta here. Bosox take a 4–3 lead here in the top of the tenth. Soothsayer Sol is filled with mirth. Red Sox Nation is filled with hope.

And when, following strikeouts by Owen and Schiraldi, Boggs doubles to the wall in left-center and Barrett singles to right, making it 5–3 Bosox, the mirth and the hope blossom into ecstasy and optimism.

Buckner leaves Barrett stranded at first, but no matter.

"Let's go, Mets!" shouts a die-hard fan behind Seth, Sol, and Janet. "It's never too late!"

Shades of '51, Seth observes, when a certain other New York ball club roared back in their last licks to snatch victory from the jaws of defeat.

"Hey, Janet?" Sol says.

"Mmm?"

"I'm sure glad we share this passion. It makes things a lot easier, you know."

"Yes, I agree, Solomon. We're two lucky people."

Seth can't believe what he's hearing. Or what he *thinks* he's hearing.

Another plane swoops past the stadium, this time on its way from the airport. The poor 287 people on that big bird who are missing all the History down here, Seth thinks.

"Three more lousy outs, and we're home!" Sol yells.

Janet flashes him a dirty look.

Seth recognizes the Bosox out there. Jim Rice 14, Dave Henderson 40, and Dwight Evans 24 pegging in the distance; Wade Boggs 26, Spike Owen 12, Marty Barrett 17, and Bill Buckner 6 on the infield dirt; Rich Gedman 10 behind the plate, catching the warm-ups of a confident-looking Calvin Schiraldi 31. Yep, only two starting African-American players. How sad.

Before another play ever happens on the field, the plot thickens. Joining Seth and Sol and Janet is a man who jostles past them to seat himself on the other side of Janet, three Buds in a cardboard holder in his hands. He keeps one, hands one to each of the other two in the party. Sol and Janet take sips of beer out of their cups as the man settles into his seat. Sol's mustache is white now, and so is Janet's, and they giggle at each other.

The man who has joined them is the poster boy for the *Sesame Street* song "One of these men is not like the others." An impressive scar running down his right cheek, a nose rendered crooked perhaps in the boxing ring, high cheekbones, an eight o'clock shadow, expensive Italian leather shoes and a double-breasted dark green suit with a solid pink shirt and a solid red tie—he has come straight out of the raucous pages of a Damon Runyon story.

"Anything happen while I was gone?" Nathan Detroit asks.

"Yeah, Hendu hit a dinger and then they scored again, so we're in a 5–3 hole with three outs left to the season," Janet answers.

"Crap!" Nathan replies, sinking down in his seat.

Seth's mind is in overdrive. *So who's this hoodlum Papa Sol's hanging out with?*

Bottom of the tenth, Mets' last chance, and the twenty thousand Bosox fans in attendance can just smell their first World Series title in sixty-eight long, excruciating years. Nineteen thousand nine hundred ninety-nine, actually, since Seth already knows better.

Wally Backman steps up to the plate with the Mets' hopes resting squarely on his brawny shoulders. Just then, Seth's attention is diverted from the action on the field to the action to his left. Papa Sol stretches his arm around Janet's back and furtively hands what appears to be a bulging envelope to Nathan Detroit.

What is going on here?, Seth wonders. *What kind of trouble has Papa Sol gotten himself into? Who is this guy?*

His bookie? His blackmailer? His rival in a love triangle? And what's in that envelope? Money? Is it a payoff for something? A bet on the game? Is Papa Sol deep in debt? Paying off Nathan to buy his silence? Does this have something, anything, to do with Papa Sol's sudden disappearance eighteen years hence?

Seth is the only attendee in the ballpark interested in a drama other than the one between the foul lines.

Before you could say, "Red Sox win the Series!" Backman hits a lazy fly to Rice in left, and Hernandez flies deep to Hendu in center. Two quick outs, and only one more to go before Beantown blows its top.

"Damn!" Janet mutters.

"Crap!" Nathan grouses.

"*Yesss!*" Sol hisses.

Seth admires the depth and the desperation of his grandfather's caring.

The Mets' last hope, Gary Carter, strides to the plate, oozing an eerie and inappropriate confidence.

In one of the most ironic exhibitions of prehatched chicken counting in baseball history, the scoreboard, in a premature inauguration, lights up:

CONGRATULATIONS RED SOX, 1986 WORLD SERIES CHAMPIONS.

Carter fouls one off, takes two pitches for balls, and, with a determined look on his face that says, "I ain't gonna make the last out, goddammit," loops a single to left.

"Now batting for Aguilera . . . Kevin Mitchell, number seven."

"C'mon, Kevin baby, keep it going," Nathan screams

with his gangster voice, his breast pocket bulging with Papa Sol's presumable moolah.

Sol flashes him a look of disgust and whispers imploringly to the pitcher, "Let's go, Calvin, one more stinken out. Just one more."

After a checked-swing foul, Mitchell lines a hanging slider to center for a single.

First and second now, and the pesky Ray Knight is due up. Nervous Red Sox fans crumple their programs or order another Bud or both.

"C'mon, Cal, one more stinken out. Just hang in there!"

Knight goes oh-and-two, and the Bosox are at long last one strike away from the elusive Grail. But pesky Ray has other plans and singles to center, scoring Carter, moving Mitchell to third, and bringing the Mets to within one measly run of tying it up.

"Now pitching for Boston . . . Bob Stanley, number forty-six."

While Stanley trudges in from the bull pen, Seth takes in the scene. He is trying not to dwell on Papa Sol's ostensibly troubling situation, whatever that might be, and to soak in History instead.

The section he's sitting in is populated almost entirely by Red Sox fans, and he watches and listens as Stanley takes his eight warm-up pitches.

Just as in his two other visits to the past, historian Seth senses the palpable atmosphere surrounding him. This time, it is an eerie combo platter, a strange mixture of the other two visits.

On the one hand, there is the paranoia and fear that were so evident to him in the Polo Grounds of the early fifties. The Sox fans at Shea are restless, with that "Oh no, not again, this *can't* be happening again" sneaking suspicion. They have lived through too many close Series calls, and many of these fans have actually suffered through them in person. The recurring roller coaster first began in '46, when the Sox were behind three games to two to the Cardinals and came back to win Game 6, only to lose Game 7, 4–3, after rallying from a 3–1 deficit. Then there was the '67 Series, with Lonborg and Yaz, when they stormed back, also against St. Louis, from a three-games-to-one hole, only to lose to Gibby, 7–2, once again in Game 7. Finally, there was the '75 fiasco, when they were trailing three games to two against the Reds, came back to win Game 6, 7–6, after being behind 6–3, only to lose Game 7 yet again, 4–3, this time after leading, 3–0.

On the other hand, there is the innocent hope still flickering at Shea, the same hope that imbued Candlestick in '62, the hope that keeps Red Sox Nation going, treading water, refusing to go under for good.

Fear and hope, strange bedfellows, Seth thinks. All these passionate fans, including Sol, who have bled and sweated and cried for their beloved team lo these many years, through all the disappointment and all the shattered dreams, still clinging to the promise of a victory. And these same fans, deep down in their rooting bones, know somehow, someway, that this time, once again, something bad's gonna happen.

But Red Sox Nation takes heart, because when all is said and done, they are acutely aware of the incontrovertible fact that they are still only one out, one cotton-pickin' out, from Heaven. From ending the *Curse* . . . of the Bam-**BI**no!

They are banking on this cheery thought as the ornery Mookie Wilson assumes his crooked stance in the batter's box.

Unbeknownst to everyone at Shea except Seth, here comes one of the greatest, grittiest pressure at bats in the entire glorious history of the National Pastime.

It's first and third and Mitchell's only ninety measly feet away from knotting the game up and Stanley's fidgeting on the mound and Mookie's fidgeting in the box and Janet and Nathan D. are fidgeting in their seats and Papa Sol is glaring intently at pitcher Stanley, willing him to get this friggin' thing over with, and Seth knows what's about to happen and it's breaking his heart.

Mookie fouls a pitch off and takes a ball and then another and he fouls off a second one and the count is now two-and-two and here we are, for a second time only one strike away from agony for Mets' fans and ecstasy for Red Sox Nation. And Mookie hits his third foul ball of the at bat and then his fourth and it's still two-and-two and we're still one strike away and the tension is as thick as Boston chowder.

"Y'know," Sol says to his two companions, "Mookie reminds me a little of a fellow named Richie Ashburn. Used to play for the Phillies when you guys were in diapers. One of the original Mets, in fact. Used to drive pitchers crazy, the way he'd stand in there on top of the plate and just keep fouling off pitches, hanging in there. He'd foul off six, eight, ten pitches, hell, he'd stay up there fouling off pitches all day and night it seemed and finally spray a single to the opposite field or squib a hit down the line or work the pitcher for a walk. Eventually, he'd find a way to get on, just like this guy up there now."

Janet and Nathan nod their heads, return to the action.

Nathan's program is mauled beyond recognition, an origami auto crash.

Seth is suffering in silence and Papa Sol is still urging Stanley on under his breath, but to no avail, because here comes the wild pitch at Mookie's knees that he somehow, magically, avoids being hit by and it gets past Gedman and rolls to the backstop and here comes Mitchell in to score and it's 5–5 and Knight makes it to second, to the Promised Land of Scoring Position.

The count is full and Mookie steps in again, ready to receive his eighth pitch from the shaken Stanley, and surprise! surprise! he fouls another ball back and then he hits foul number six just past third. And now he is ready for the tenth pitch of the at-bat and he bends over the plate, this dark-skinned, modern-day Richie Ashburn, and he swipes at the ball and barely tops it and here comes that world-famous little squibber of all squibbers tapped down the first-base line, that puny, measly, wretched, pathetic little bleeder of a ground ball that Seth alone in the universe knows about now but in three seconds billions will be talking about until the end of recorded time.

And everyone in Shea is standing and millions are standing up in their homes in front of their TVs and everyone is holding their collective breaths and praying, the Mets fans for one lucky break to happen and the Red Sox fans for the misery of sixty-eight long years of famine to end mercifully, and here comes the fleet Mookie sprinting down the line and Knight, he's chugging toward third and there's old Billy Buck, bum ankle and all, in the twilight of his career, in his eighteenth season and bad gam and all he's still the best-fielding first sacker you'll ever see with the possible exceptions of Gil Hodges and Don Mattingly and Keith Hernandez and Wes Parker and maybe you can throw ol' flamboyant Vic Power in there and Buckner is bending down now with his hobbled old legs to suck up the grounder like a timeworn but reliable Hoover . . .

And at this very instant, at this momentous, historical instant, Solomon Stein, who is standing a mere fifty feet or so from the ears of William Joseph Buckner, yells out, with passion, gusto, and the very best of intentions, "You *got* it, Billy boy!"

Seth is watching the play closely and already knows the outcome. But what he doesn't know and now learns—*from a historical perspective*—is that, simultaneous with Sol's outburst, Billy Buck, the split second before the ball slithers tragically between his legs, lifts his head back barely, imperceptibly, not even a millimeter, and turns it slightly to the left, toward the stands, in the direction of where the sudden vocal outburst originated from, in the direction of rabid Red Sox fan Solomon Stein. Back and to the left . . . back and to the left . . . back and to the left . . .

Knight scores the winning run from second and Mets fans are raising their arms to heaven, hugging and kissing one another, jumping up and down and sideways, screaming, yelling, *hoo-ha*ing, ranting, raving, flipping out, going bonkers and bananas and nuts.

Sox fans are silent as tombs, mouths open, hands scratching heads or wringing themselves or making fists or slapping cheeks. The shock of *oh no, not again!* has just begun to set in.

Solomon Stein is frozen by his guilt, the sense that maybe, maybe, even quite possibly, he was in part responsible for Buckner's unforgivable gaffe. The sense of shame, etched on his drawn, wan face, is even stronger than the grief of watching his Bosox blow it big-time. He knows in his gut that this game has *two* goats.

Seth watches Papa Sol with feelings of pity and fear and love.

Pity, for a man who, to Seth's knowledge and maybe more often than that, has now three times in his life been the major participant in a fall from ecstasy to despair: the Giants' pennant victory followed by the Ball Fiasco, the hope of a Giants' World Series victory followed by the Taunt that Backfired, and now *this,* the Red Sox being one strike away from a World Series triumph, followed by the Disaster of the Open Wickets.

Fear, for a man who, on top of all his prior disappointments and God knows what other ones and now *this,* probably still has that .38 pistol stashed away somewhere.

Love, for a man who, above and beyond the above, has always showered unconditional love on Seth, come rain or come shine.

Nathan Detroit and Janet and the other 35,076 Mets fans are hoopin' and hollerin' and going wild, while 19,999 of the Red Sox fans are standing in stony silence, still smarting from the force of the ton of bricks that just hit them.

Red Sox fan number 20,000 is sitting in his seat, next to his grandson, tears of grief streaming down his cheeks and vanishing into his beard.

This is the first time Seth has ever seen his grandfather cry.

Seth is numb from the drama, from witnessing Papa Sol's despair. Although he knows the gesture will go unheeded, he places his right hand on his grandfather's right bicep, gives it a gentle squeeze.

"It's okay, Papa Sol. It's okay . . ."

". . . it's okay, Papa Sol."

Seth is standing to the side of Solomon Stein, who, deaf to his grandson's consoling words, is sitting alone in the living room of his Cambridge house. It is just past midnight. A *Boston Globe* hangs limply in Papa Sol's trembling carpenter's hands. He is looking at a black-and-white blowup of the hapless Bill Buckner, between whose hobbled legs the infamous Mookie Wilson squibber is oozing. A photo that is now appearing in millions of newspapers and magazines across the nation. A photo, Seth speculates, that in time will rank right up there in the annals of Americana along with the snapshots of the Babe bowing out at Yankee Stadium, the devastation at Pearl Harbor, the triumph at Iwo Jima, the spontaneous V-J Day kiss, Ruby shooting Oswald, the brutally cold Viet Cong pistol execution, man's first exhilarating steps on the moon, and the two towers burning on September 11.

"You *got* it, Billy boy!" Papa Sol repeats twice, slowly, with profound regret and excruciating sarcasm.

All Seth can think about is the humility that baseball— this game Sol adores and worships and that has given him so much pleasure—has once again burdened his grandfather with.

And where the hell that .38 is stashed.

Instinctively, he puts his right hand on the back of Papa Sol's neck and squeezes it. Maybe he can somehow massage the pain and the depression away?

Sol is still looking at his paper, shaking his head, oblivious to Seth's gesture of commiseration. Seth continues, anyway, squeezing the back of Papa Sol's neck, rubbing it, kneading it, kneading . . .

⚾

In his Cambridge study, Seth is kneading a scuffed baseball with his right hand. He opens his eyes extra wide, shakes off the cobwebs, places the ball back in the green-felt safety of its niche, closes the box.

He is sitting in his La-Z-Boy, and his brain is in fifth gear, a succession of thoughts from this last trip floating out of his head like a string of soap bubbles, then popping, one by one, in the air above him.

He is thinking about a quote he brought up in class the other day, from the Danish philosopher Søren Kierkegaard:

Life must be lived forward, but it can only be understood backward.

About how privileged he is to be experiencing History, to be learning, little by little, about the untold story of his Papa Sol, to be understanding life better by traveling backward in his dual roles of grandson and historian.

He is thinking about another quote, this one from former baseball announcer Hank Greenwald:

Has anyone ever satisfactorily explained why the bad hop is always the last one?

About the wisdom and the irony of this rhetorical question as it relates to Mookie's grounder that probably ruined the life of Bill Buckner and possibly those of millions of Bosox fans, the grounder that never took its expected last hop, that to Buckner's surprise somehow hugged the ground and never hopped at all. About bad hops in general and how they are metaphors for bad breaks and misfortune, in sports and in life, and how they can be devastating or recovered from. About History's slender thread, the fine line that separates winners from losers, the thin sliver of difference that could have allowed Buckner to retire with a Series ring but instead made him and ignominy lifelong partners, the same sliver that made Bobby Thomson, Carlton Fisk, Doug Flutie, Franco Harris, Keith Smart, Christian Laettner, and Lorenzo Charles heroes, and Ralph Branca, Fred Merkle, Mickey Owen, Roberto De Vicenzo, Chris Webber, Jackie Smith, and Donnie Moore goats.

He is thinking about injustice and how unfair life after baseball was to Branca and Buckner, two of the good guys. About the injustice of things that happened in Papa Sol's life, things that Seth has now witnessed firsthand: the invalid ball, the taunt that backfired, the Buckner bungle. From the injustice index card file in his brain, Seth plucks a few choice quotations. One from RFK:

Justice delayed is democracy denied.

And then one from Jules Renard:

There is a justice, but we do not always see it. Discreet, smiling, it is there, at one side, a little behind injustice, which makes a big noise.

And a third from Mets journeyman Rod Kanehl:

Baseball is a lot like life. The line drives are caught, the squibbers go for base hits. It's an unfair game.

About the historical fact that in the Preamble to the Constitution, the seventeenth of the fifty-two words is *Justice.* And of the six powers of the new government (more perfect Union, Justice, Tranquility, defense, Welfare, Liberty), Justice is the first specific power mentioned. *So why does it seem to happen so rarely in America?*

He is thinking about the Greek poet Pindar and one of his odes that might as well be describing the remainder of Billy Buck's ill-fated life:

> . . . *the loser's hateful return, the jeering voices, the furtive back alleys . . .*

He is thinking about Aristotle and his classical definition of Tragedy. Mookie's squibber, and what it did to Billy Buck's life, has made him think of this. From an undergrad philosophy course, he recalls, word for word, a number of the aspects of the definition, aspects that, in some strange and disquieting way, define Buckner himself as a tragic figure. Tragedy being an action that is "serious, complete in itself, and of an adequate magnitude." Tragedy cathartically arousing "the emotions of pity and fear in the audience," pity being "what we feel at a misfortune that is out of proportion to the faults of a man" and fear being "what we feel when misfortune comes upon one like ourselves." Tragedy making men "happy or miserable in their actual deeds." Tragedy imitating incidents that "affect us most powerfully when we are not expecting them." Tragedy happening not to "a man whose misfortune comes about through vice and depravity" but to "a man who is brought low through some error of judgment or shortcoming." Tragedy being a change of fortune that is "a fall from happiness to misery."

How troubling to consider that the Greek philosopher might just as well have been thinking of Bill Buckner as of Oedipus. Buckner, a good man who led a good life and whose lifetime stats were barely below Hall of Fame levels—twenty-two seasons, over twenty-five hundred games, nearly ten thousand at bats, 1,077 runs, 2,715 hits, a .289 career BA, and a .992 career fielding percentage. And one little bleeder between his legs, and that's all he'll ever be remembered for, that and his subsequent self-exile to a little town outside of Boise, Idaho. How troubling, too, for Seth to consider that there might have been something tragic, in this same Aristotelian sense, about the life of his Papa Sol, who must have carried around all that baggage with him, all by himself and for all those years.

He is thinking about the look on Papa Sol's face as his grandfather stared at the Buckner blowup in the *Globe,* the same troubled look as the one he saw at the Polo Grounds and the one he saw in the basement pistol scene and the one he saw after the Ralph Terry fiasco, but this one even more intense. What demons had been lurking inside Papa Sol? What forces had been making him hide his secrets from his loved ones? What black clouds had been gathering above his head, waiting to erupt in a potential thunderstorm of self-eradication? Was Papa Sol, this loving and wonderful but flawed human being, living, like his beloved Bosox, under some horrible *Curse?* Did he have sufficient motive for ending his own life? The ball? The taunt? Buckner's blunder? A gambling problem? Money woes? The shame and guilt of adultery? Something else even more pernicious? Is Seth closer to deducing any of this, to answering his many questions about what happened to his grandfather? Or did this last visit just raise more questions?

He is thinking about why and how all this is occurring, why and how the baseball is bringing him back to the past to see the unexplored sides of his Papa Sol. Has it all been real, or, despite the prima facie evidence, has it been a dream? Is the discovery of Papa Sol's secrets worth the complications, the unpleasantness, the sadness? Are the quest for the truth and the true study of History—White-head's "nerves and vitals"—worth all the pain?

Seth looks up, and his eyes focus on something on his desk, a simple object that abruptly terminates his string of thoughts. It is a coffee mug that Kate presented to him on his last birthday. It says:

EVERY
THING
HAPPENS

FOR A REASON

5

BUMP

Kate Richman
Ms. Kate Richman
Kate Stein
Ms. Kate Stein
Mrs. Kate Stein
Kate Ellen Stein
Ms. Kate Ellen Stein
Mrs. Kate Ellen Stein
Kate Richman Stein
Ms. Kate Richman Stein
Mrs. Kate Richman Stein
Kate Richman-Stein
Ms. Kate Richman-Stein
Mrs. Kate Richman-Stein
Kate Ellen Richman Stein
Ms. Kate Ellen Richman Stein
Mrs. Kate Ellen Richman Stein
Kate Ellen Richman-Stein
Ms. Kate Ellen Richman-Stein
Mrs. Kate Ellen Richman-Stein

LOOKS LIKE A GODDAM CHRISTMAS TREE, Kate is thinking.

"Watcha doin', sweetie pie?" Seth yells from the bedroom.

"Oh, nothing, just doodling, honey," Kate answers as she crumples up her dreams into a tight little paper wad and tosses them in the garbage pail under the sink.

Seth makes his grand entrance to Kate's kitchen, freshly showered, barefoot, and wearing a pair of ratty jeans and a crimson T-shirt with a white HARVARD on the front, under which the word **VERITAS** is printed inside a white crest. His thick hair is disheveled and still moist.

He loves the fact that of the some 616,500 words in the English language, *truth* (and in Latin, no less) was the one carefully selected as a motto by his university.

"So then, Mum, which of your distinctive wines shall we quaff to prepare our palates for this evening's victuals?" Seth asks, with his Dickensian accent.

Kate looks at her cherished oenological holdings, which, resting on their backs, recline in an attractive twelve-bottle teak rack in the corner of the counter. There's a 2005 Orvieto, awaiting the next chicken piccata; a nice Pinot Grigio she uses for reduction sauces; a lovely 2003 Sancerre; four respectable bottles of Penfolds 2002 Koonunga Hill Shiraz Cabernet; a magnificent 2001 Bluegrass Cab from New South Wales; two divine 2003 Santa Ynez Valley Nebbiolos; a delectable 1996 Château Olivier Graves; and a nec plus ultra Cavallotto Barolo she's been saving for a rainy day.

"I'm feeling a little 'country' this evening, so let's have the Bluegrass," Kate chortles, rousting the Aussie Cab they'd purchased on a trip to Down Under from its cozy bed and depositing it on the counter for Seth's approval.

Seth eyes the label, wrings his hands, purses his lips, and scrunches his eyes into narrow slits, crow's-feet forming at the corners. "Yes, that'll do us quite nicely, Miss Agnes, quite nicely indeed," he intones unctuously, attempting his Uriah Heep imitation. "It looks like an *umble* wine, if you ask me, and being an *umble* person meself, it'll do us quite nicely."

Seth opens the bottle, pours a half inch into his own glass, swirls it, sniffs it, then guzzles it down like a parched caveman, the pinky of his right hand pointing straight up to the firmament.

"Why yes, dear Agnes," he says, with a mischievous smile, "it'll do us quite nicely, this most *umble* of wines."

Charles Dickens, wine, and cooking are three of Seth and Kate's shared passions (there's also tennis, music, acoustic guitar, art history, gardening, animals, poetry, and the Red Sox) that are conspiring to make this evening special.

Kate turns the heat on the stove down to a low flame, stirs the ingredients in the large frying pan with a thick wooden spoon purchased in Concarneau, Brittany, puts on the cover. Tonight's feast—to be served over squid ink tagliatelle pasta—will be *poulet à la flamande,* a recipe she picked up during her junior year in Antwerp from a couple she'd befriended, the Dunkelblums on Belgielei. It is a tender, stewy dish, in which chicken parts are dredged in flour, then slowly cooked in an ever-thickening potion of onions, garlic, prunes, bay leaves, seasoning, apple cider vinegar, Dijon mustard spread on wheat bread, and, most essential, two oversize bottles of outrageous Chimay Belgian ale. The ingredients are just beginning their ninety-minute simmering sojourn to perfection.

"Shall we repair to the drawing room, my love?" Kate asks. The two clink glasses, take a swig, exchange adoring looks, and amble to more comfortable quarters.

Kate's living room is small but tastefully decorated. Prints by Picasso, Blake, Rembrandt, and Ronald Searle. The cooking diplomas and chef's hat picture. Light green sofa. Teak-and-glass coffee table, on which rests a delicate, goosenecked, yellow-and-gray-striped Kosta Boda vase with three fresh daisies peeking out. Contemporary Swedish rocker.

And her desk, her workplace, so neat and tidy. In-box. Out-box. Neat little pile of typed recipes. Pencils and pens lined up evenly. Maroon Filofax. Tensor lamp. And, wedged between black metal bookends and arranged by title in alphabetical order, a tasty collection of some of the great classical cookbooks: *De re coquinaria* by Apicius, *El Cocinero Puertorriqueño, Larousse Gastronomique,* Artusi's *La scienza in cucina e l'arte di mangiar bene, The Alice B. Toklas Cookbook*, and, of course, *The Closet of the Eminently Learned Sir Kenelme Digby Kt. Opened.* Everything in its rightful, premeditated place.

Kate is Felix to Seth's Oscar.

In unison, Kate and Seth clink and take a second sip of the Bluegrass as they snuggle on the sofa. *Mmmmm.*

On cue, Billy Joel is singing "Scenes from an Italian Restaurant," the part about bottle of red. Billy is the first cut on their favorite eclectic CD mix, which also includes tunes by Fred Astaire, Gershwin, Randy Newman, Dixie Chicks, the Beatles, the Eagles, Alison Krauss, Indigo Girls, Jackson Browne, Seals & Crofts, Alain Souchon, Joe Cocker, Van Morrison, Francesco De Gregori, Kathy Mattea, Billie Holiday, Karla Bonoff, Phil Collins, Christine McVie, Gino

Paoli, James Taylor, Roberto Vecchioni, Elton John, Georges Brassens, Jacques Brel, and Ella.

"So how was your day, sweetie?" Kate asks.

"Oh, pretty hectic actually," Seth says. "Beat Gordon in a tight one this morning. Prepared a pretty interesting class for tomorrow, all about *passion.*"

Kate gives Seth one of those Mae West "Why dontcha come up and see me sometime?" glances. Seth returns it with one of those Jimmy Cagney "Aw, simmer down, sister, or else you'll get a juicy grapefruit right in the puss" looks.

"And, let's see, worked on the book a little, then made a date with one of my gorgeous, hot students."

Kate's ears become a Doberman's, perking up at the hint of a suspected prowler.

"Just wanted to see if you were paying attention, sweetie pie."

Kate is not amused.

"Anyway, it was a damn good day, if I don't say so myself," Seth concludes, taking his third sip. "And yours?"

"Oh, me? Thanks for asking, dear," Kate answers, with playful sarcasm. "It was pretty crappy, truth be told. Frédéric, that new *chef de cuisine* I told you about? Well, he chose me and Samantha to do a 'cook-off' to see whose omelette recipe he'll be serving on the new menu."

"So you made the finals. What's so crappy about that?"

"I'll tell you what's so crappy. Frédéric tasted my omelette, smiled sweetly, told me how he adored my cooking. Then he tasted Sam's omelette, smiled sweetly, cracked some dumb joke, something like, 'but I only have thyme for you,' and chose hers."

"That little bitch!"

"Yeah, can you believe it?" Kate says, welling up.

"Listen, Kate, you are the absolute best, don't you know that? Best cook, best lover, best person in the world. Forget about Samantha," Seth consoles, muttering *"that little bitch!"* again under his breath.

Kate's anger melts, and she cracks up, puts her arms around Seth, hugs him tight, plants a smoldering kiss on his unsuspecting mouth.

"You'll show 'em, babe, don't you worry!" Seth says, raising his glass.

"I propose . . . ," he says, smiling at Kate wryly, milking the double entendre.

Kate glares at Seth, then, correcting herself, cracks up again and picks up her glass. She feels the warmth of the wine and of Seth, and a golden glow emanates from her face, like the one surrounding the angel's face in Duccio's painting *Annunciation of the Death of the Virgin.*

". . . a toast," Seth continues, "to the most beautiful, most intelligent, most talented, most loving woman I've ever known."

Kate loses it, and a lone projectile tear leaps into her glass. She cracks up a third time.

Another simultaneous sip. Love is in the air.

"I know things are gonna turn out just fine, my sweet," Seth says. "Speaking of which, you know that coffee mug you gave me?"

"You mean the one with Woody Allen's quote 'Eternity is long, especially toward the end'?"

"No. I love that one, but I mean the mug you gave me a while ago for my birthday. The one that says—"

" 'Everything happens for a reason,' " Kate interrupts.

"Yeah. Well, I've been thinking about that. A lot, actually. Do you believe those words?"

"Mmm . . . yeah, I guess. I mean, I do think that maybe

out there somewhere, somehow, there's a plan for us. Things don't always work out as we'd like, or at least they don't *seem* to. Then one day, they do, and everything makes sense again."

Another synchronous sip, and now it's Seth's turn.

"I agree. Take this thing at the restaurant. Maybe Samantha's not such a little bitch, y'know? Maybe she's as good as Frédéric thinks she is. That doesn't mean you're not as good as, or even better than, she is. But objectively speaking? Maybe now's not the exact time you're supposed to be 'the Chosen One.' And maybe we don't know now what that reason is, but that doesn't mean there isn't one, right?"

"I s'pose. Yeah, well, thanks for making me feel a *little* better."

They kiss, take another sip.

"Sweetie, why are you thinking about this now? Something happen to *you*?"

"Nah. Well," Seth answers, then, reflecting, "yeah, something *did* happen, a few times—"

"Wanna tell me about it?"

"Sure. It's just that, well, Kate . . . I've been seeing . . . Papa Sol."

Dead silence.

"You mean you've been dreaming—"

"No . . . well, maybe . . . I dunno. Yeah, probably in my dreams. But it all seems so real, and then there was the stub and—"

"Whoa. Slow down, honey. The stub?"

"A ticket stub, from a baseball game I think I went to and saw Papa Sol at—"

"So? It could've been—"

"It was to a game that was played before I was born—"

"But, honey, you could've found it at Elsie's and—"

"Well, maybe. Anyway, I'm not sure if it was a dream or not, but I've seen sides to Papa Sol I never saw before. And I saw things happen to him that must've made him very sad. Sad enough to . . ."

Seth doesn't ever remember crying as an adult. Ever. And he's not about to start now. He takes a deep breath, collects himself.

"I love you, Seth Stein."

"I love you, Kate Richman."

"So," Seth adds, "I've just been thinking lately about all these things and about how they must happen for a reason. Maybe we don't see that reason, but it must be there. Because if it's not, then life can be pretty damn sad or meaningless or desperate or—"

"I *love* you, Seth Stein," Kate whispers again, placing her right hand behind Seth's neck, massaging his nape.

"*Aaaaah.* You are *goooood.*"

Kate gets up, checks the *flamande,* stirs it twice, replaces the cover.

"About forty-five minutes till it's ready, honey pie," Kate announces, returning from the kitchen. Seth gives Kate that look. Kate returns it.

Now the two are lying in the bed, their warm bodies pressed together. Seth slides the fingertips of his left hand down Kate's soft, arched back, slowly, stealthily, luringly, lustily.

Fade to black.

①

"Ladies and gentlemen . . ."

"Dr. Stein . . ."

"Today, as advertised, we're going to be discussing the historical concept of *passion*. Now, you all know what passion is, don't you?"

General tittering and nodding, except for Libby Frank, who shakes her head, and exchange student Sylvie Corbière, who turns red as a *betterave*.

"Okay, settle down, guys. Now, to begin with, we're not talking about the kind of passion you might experience in, say, the backseat of a Honda. Or screaming at Fenway when you're rooting for the Bosox. Does anyone know where the word *passion* comes from?"

Predictably, Stephanie Lowell's arm zooms skyward.

"Yes, it's from the Latin *pati,* to suffer."

"Also from the Greek *pathein,* same meaning," Bronson Larrabee IV adds.

"Excellent!" Seth says. "And so, we're talking about the fact that passion, in a historical sense, is about the suffering of the past, the struggles and toil and travail that are the crucibles for action and achievement. I'd like to read the quote from Churchill I gave you to think about last class, just to refresh your memories." Seth assumes a close-lipped, dropped-chin, lower-register, upper-crust British accent:

> *History with its flickering lamp stumbles along the trail of the past, trying to reconstruct its scenes, to revive its echoes, and kindle with pale gleams the passion of former days.*

"Ostensibly, Churchill was speaking about his just-deceased predecessor, Neville Chamberlain, in an attempt to soften his Hitler-appeasing stance, with which Churchill so vehemently disagreed. But on a deeper level, Churchill, who had lived through many historical events himself, must have been thinking of something a lot more profound. So, what do you suppose he was getting at, and what do you think he meant by *passion*?"

The class is pensive, soaking it all in, delaying the signal between left brain and right arm. Finally, it is Donna Hemming, a bright, athletic young lady with short brown hair and intense green eyes, who is the first to respond.

"I think he's basically saying that History is a failure. I mean, he says it 'tries to' reconstruct the past and that it 'stumbles along.' The past is sort of like a photo you take, and when it's new, it's clear and colorful, but then as time goes by, it fades, and History can't really put back the color in it."

"Well said," Seth says. "And *passion*?"

"Wait just a second," Libby Frank protests. "I'm not sure he meant that History is a failure. After all, wasn't he a lifelong student of History? Didn't he live it, write about it? I doubt he wanted to *diss* History altogether. Maybe he was just being modest?"

"Could be," Seth agrees. "Yes, I don't think Churchill would see History as a total failure. So then, what do you think he meant by *passion*?"

"I think he meant the same thing as Whitehead meant by 'nerves and vitals.' That is, what *really* went down, the inside story, what people were feeling," Stephanie answers. "And like Donna said, this passion tends to fade in time, and the historian has a bitch of a job putting the flame back."

"Okay, good," Seth says. "So now, let's be more specific. Can you think of some passion of the past—deep feelings that defined a historical event—that once burned bright and that now we, as historians, have to try to 'reconstruct,' 'revive,' and 'kindle'?"

Seth's mind takes a momentary sabbatical from the class, wandering back to his visits with Papa Sol. Churchill's quote has inspired him to reflect on how he, and he alone in the history of mankind, has been able to walk down "the trail of the past," to reconstruct some of the key scenes of Papa Sol's existence, to revive the echoes of his mute calls for help, to kindle the true passion his grandfather felt toward life and baseball and that, during his life, he had revealed fully to no one.

"How about the Holocaust?" the usually timid Josh Greenfield answers, jolting Seth from his reverie.

"The Holocaust," Seth echoes, coming to.

"I mean," Josh says, with feeling, "there were six million Jews eradicated, and five million others, and yet the passion of that experience is fading a little bit every passing day. How can people ever forget the 'passion' of that monster Hitler? How can they forget all the human suffering and despair? The families torn apart? I lost my great-grandfather at Auschwitz, so the memory of his 'passion' lives on in our family. But for most people, the Holocaust was horrible, yes, but it has become a distant memory. And some people, fanatics like that Iranian piece of crap, Ahmadinejad, are just in denial that it ever happened! Listen, thank God for the Simon Wiesenthals and the Elie Wiesels of the world, who have kept reminding us that, even though time can make our memory of these events fuzzy, we can't allow ourselves to forget. There's a Hebrew word, *nizkor*, that means 'we will remember.' And we *have* to. 'The passion of former days' cannot die. If it does, we're totally *screwed*."

Wow.

"Beautifully expressed, Josh," Seth says to his flock, piercing through the awed silence of the lambs.

Jamaal Crosby makes the same point about remembering the civil rights movement, Libby Frank tosses in feminism, Maria Lopez makes a plea not to forget the good works of César Chávez.

Just now, Seth Stein has a nearly uncontrollable urge to scream out his confession, like the narrator at the end of Poe's harrowing tale "The Tell-Tale Heart":

> *I admit the deed! 'Twas I who visited Papa Sol in his past; 'twas I alone who walked along the dusty trails of the past, a true historian, seeing things not with a flickering lamp, but with a flaming torch! Yes, just as you suspected . . . 'twas I!*

Instead, Seth says to his minions, "I guess the question here is not whether History deserves to be remembered, but whether it *can* be. Yes, Sylvie?"

Drop-dead, sultry beauty Sylvie Corbière, the exchange student from Nantes with the impeccable pseudo-British accent, opines, "I have to agree with the great writer Marcel Proust here. The present dies the minute it is born, and it cannot be recaptured easily, if at all. I do not think that History can do this job adequately. As Proust thought, only art, in the form of the carefully written word, can reconstruct the past."

Seth's entire professional future on the planet is in imminent danger of collapsing.

"I agree to a certain extent with that thesis," he responds, "but writing is only words, beautiful words perhaps, but words nonetheless. Has anyone heard the Latin expression *facta non verba*?"

"Deeds, not words," Bronson Larrabee IV translates.

"Yes. The two are quite different, of course. It is the *deeds* of the past that we, as historians, are interested in, not just describing them, but *reliving* them."

Phew. Close call, but Seth's career is back on track.

"Karen?"

Karen Fink, the stately, articulate blonde sitting directly across the table from Seth, speaks. "I was just going to agree with Sylvie."

Oy.

"We studied the poem 'Ozymandias' last week for an English course, and I think Shelley would agree with Proust," Karen says, reading from a book she has removed from her backpack.

Half sunk a shattered visage lies, whose frown,
And wrinkled lip, and sneer of cold command,
Tell that its sculptor well those passions read
Which yet survive, stamped on those lifeless things,
The hand that mocked them, and the heart that fed . . .

"I think the poet was saying that statues and objects and anything that becomes the past will naturally decay and disappear—in the poem, he mentions 'two vast and trunkless legs of stone,' a 'shattered visage,' and 'the decay of that colossal Wreck'—and that the only thing that endures forever is 'passions,' in this case the spirit of ruthlessness of the king, Ozymandias, that the sculptor captured beneath the stone of the statue. These passions survive even the sculptor's hand, and it is art, like Proust's writing, that alone can attempt to resuscitate the past."

Seth is imagining that he will be eternally damned to a life of unemployment.

Mercifully, the bloodbath is saved by the bell.

"This has been a very stimulating discussion, guys," he says. "Whether art and literature alone can preserve the past, or History, with its attempt to put the pieces of what really happened together—the answer to this burning question will sadly have to wait until the next time we meet. Thank you, all."

A warm round of applause, and the students rise and begin to file out.

Seth is envisioning Papa Sol in his old armchair, his anthology of Romantic poems clasped in his carpenter's hands. Perhaps he is reading "Ozymandias"?

Seth collects his index cards, pen, and books, tosses them in his briefcase, puts on his parka and, finally, his baseball cap.

Stephanie Lowell is the last student to leave. As she passes Seth, she pirouettes, looks at him, and says, "Great class. New haberdasher?"

Huh?

❍

Seth turns the key in the door of his town house, enters, takes off his parka and cap, throws them on the floor.

So where did Stephanie learn the word *haberdasher?* And what did she mean by her remark?

He goes to the bathroom for a pee and a quick washup, dries his hands, walks back to the study, and settles into his La-Z-Boy.

He sits and mulls, and his eyes drift over to the pile of clothes on the floor next to him, particularly to his baseball cap. Something is different. He wears his trusty cap virtually every day of his life, and something is definitely different.

He looks at the back of the cap, and he realizes that its

color is not the familiar navy blue of his Red Sox cap, but a lighter blue, a . . . *Dodgers blue*. He picks the cap up, studies it, turns it around. On the front, he discovers not the familiar red **B** of his Bosox cap, but an orange **NY**, the letters interlocked, the font pilfered from the old Giants. He is holding in his trembling hands not his Boston Red Sox cap, but a New York Mets cap, the kind you might buy at the ballpark.

Egad.

First the stub, then the mustard stain, then the sunburn, now the Mets cap. Screw Shelley and Proust. Long live *History*!

Seth had had a melancholy walk back home from Robinson and his two o'clock class. Thinking of the holes Sylvie and Karen had poked in Seth Stein's Grand Theory of History. Thinking of Grandma Elfie and hoping she wasn't too sad today. Thinking of Papa Sol and all the conflict he must have endured during his life. But now, because of this mounting pile of evidence, he feels validated, energized, optimistic, cheery. In fact, this calls for a victory cigar.

He opens the humidor sitting on his desk, selects a stogie he's been saving for just this sort of occasion—a large, 178-millimeter Cohiba Esplendidos. He clips the tip and lights up.

Ahhhhh.

Like savoring Balvenie, appreciating primo cigars is another treasured baton Papa Sol had passed on to Seth. How to clip them. How to light them. How to hold them. How to draw in the smoke, roll it around his mouth, exhale it smoothly. How to blow smoke rings, big ones, small ones, still smaller ones that can be expelled through their predecessors.

Seth is fashioning exquisite little smoke rings while

Fred Astaire croons the old classic "The Way You Look Tonight" in the background. The Jerome Kern music, the Dorothy Fields lyrics, and the mellow, high-pitched genius that is Fred's magical voice all make Seth think of his lovely Kate, and the way she'll look tonight, too.

Feeling debonair, Seth hauls his behind out of the La-Z-Boy and onto the dance floor. He floats around the study, his feet light as a feather, with an imaginary Kate who is impersonating an imaginary Ginger, the fingertips of his right hand barely grazing his invisible partner's bare upper back—his cigar is wedged between the index and middle fingers—and those of his left delicately resting on her right hand, holding it tenderly, as they would hold a Riedel wineglass or a Stradivarius.

As Fred croons about wrinkled noses and foolish hearts, Seth dances gracefully around the coffee table, then the desk, and gives Kate an affectionate, imaginary peck on the cheek. Now he sways back and forth with Kate's ghost, and they do one of those Fred-and-Ginger shoulder fakes, change direction, circle the desk again, and, out of the corner of his left eye, Seth spies Papa Sol's carved wooden box.

The music continues, but the dancing stops.

Seth releases invisible Kate, picks up the box, and returns to his La-Z-Boy.

Now, more than ever, he wants to go back again to visit Papa Sol, to see him once more, to put an end to the mystery and the secrets, to answer, once and for all, all the questions.

He opens the box, removes the ball, grips it tight. He leans back in his La-Z-Boy, puts his cigar in its ashtray, places his arms at his sides. He is ready for liftoff.

Nothing.

Seth squeezes the ball again, but still nothing. Huh? What's up? Did I do something wrong? How come nothing's—

¡Ay, caramba!

Room spins, *Dah-de-lah-de-lah*, calm, Beatles, Slide Show.

The invention of coins by the Lydians and Caesar's assassination and the Hundred Years War and Joan of Arc being burned at the stake at Rouen and Gutenberg's printing press and Newton studying gravity and Grant and Lee at Appomattox and Marie and Pierre Curie discover radium and Einstein's Theory of Relativity and the UN is formed and the fall of the Berlin Wall and Dolly the sheep is cloned . . .

And the final burst of the Beatles' riff and the rousing, raucous, brash, clashing, strident, high-pitched, piercing, trumpety climax. And the tornado grinds to a halt. And Seth is deposited gently on the ground. It is no longer 2006.

⟨℃⟩

It is 2004.

Seth knows it is, because he is looking at a big, fancy clock sitting on a glass living-room coffee table. The digital clock is made of silver and dark wood. It says 5:13 P.M. Above the time is the inscription:

To Papa Sol. With Love, Setharoo.

Below the time is the date, spelled out in gorgeous serif letters:

Oct. 19 2004

The date is ringing a bell for Seth, and as soon as his head clears, the bell becomes a gong: This was the last day anyone ever saw Papa Sol, the anyone being Sammy and Elsie and Kate and Seth. Not only that, but it is his thirty-first birthday.

Seth hears laughter. He follows its ripples, which lead him to the roomy kitchen in the Cambridge home of Papa Sol and Grandma Elsie. Celebrating at the kitchen table are seventy-six-year-old Solomon Stein, seventy-five-year-old Elsie Stein, ten-year-old Sammy Stein, twenty-eight-year-old Kate Richman, and thirty-one-year-old Seth Stein.

Seth Stein, the birthday boy.

This time around, for thirty-three-year-old Seth the interloper, the party is every bit as joyous as it was two years ago.

And everyone is singing "For He's a Jolly Good Fellow" and Kate marches in with a birthday cake she baked out of love in the form of a white baseball with red stitches and HAPPY 31ST, SETH! written in script and Seth blows out all thirty-one candles in a single breath and Sammy giggles and there are stories all around told by Sol to Seth and Seth to Sammy and Sol to Sammy and Sammy to Sol and also singing and laughter and Elfie and Kate are bonding and now Sammy's got icing all over the tip of his nose and everyone cracks up and Seth wipes Sammy's nose and they look each other right in the eyes and Sammy hugs Seth and says happy birthday Dad I love you and all that crap between Seth and Julie and Sammy melts away into nothingness.

It's like a snapshot of happiness frozen in time, and older Seth is getting to live it all over again. He smiles at the thought that if Dickens were writing a novel about this moment in time, he'd call it *A Tale of One City,* and the opening sentence would be:

It was the best of times.

Amid the celebration and the mirth, as Seth watches his younger self and his loved ones having the time of their lives, a disturbing thought occurs to him: *This is the eve of the day Papa Sol disappeared and the last time any of us ever saw him.* This time around, returning to this evening, looking in from the outside as an objective historian, would he notice any signs, any hints, any harbingers, any inklings that might give him a clue regarding Sol's disappearance?

During a rare lull in the festivities, birthday boy Seth and Papa Sol find themselves in a corner of the kitchen, chatting, a cup of coffee in each of their right hands. Older Seth listens in.

"So, Papa Sol, you gonna be watching the Big Game tomorrow?" birthday boy asks.

"You crazy? Seventh game of the ALCS? Bosox and Yanks? Winner goes to the Series? *I wouldn't miss it for the world!*"

Sol winks that mischievous wink.

"You think the Bosox'll really do it, beat those damn Yankees?" Seth asks.

"Of course, they will. I mean, ya gotta have faith. That's what being a Sox fan is all about, just like I taught you. And the odds are with them. No one's ever come back from three games down to sweep the next four in a playoff series, so it's about time."

"Not in baseball, anyway," well-schooled Seth says. "There were the '42 Leafs and the '75 Islanders in hockey. But never in baseball."

"Right you are, Setharoo!" Papa Sol says proudly. "Not until tomorrow, that is!"

"The *New York Times* says tomorrow is Mickey Mantle's birthday and the day after is Whitey Ford's birthday and that's a sign that the Yanks can't lose," Seth says.

"Well, whaddya expect a New York rag to say, huh? Mark my words, Setharoo, our Sox are gonna do it! And I'll be right there with 'em, you can bet your sweet bippee."

Seth the interloper wipes his eyes with a Happy Birthday napkin.

◖⬤◗

Seth opens his eyes and finds himself sitting next to seventy-six-year-old Papa Sol at yet a fourth historic baseball game. The contest, not yet begun, is the deciding ALCS Game 7 between the beloved Red Sox and the damn Yankees. Seth knows it is, because there are the 2004 Yanks on the field, in their pinstripes, A-Rod and Jeter and Cairo and Clark, then Matsui and Bernie and Sheffield, and Posada behind the plate and Kevin Brown on the mound, and Red Sox Johnny Damon swinging a few bats and getting ready to walk up to the plate.

And here is Seth, beside Papa Sol, sitting down the left-field line in the most hallowed of all baseball parks. Since opening its doors in 1923, the host of thirty-seven World Series matchups. The site of Babe's sixtieth homer in '27, Gehrig's farewell address in '39 and Ruth's in '48, Larsen's perfecto in '56, Maris's sixty-first in '61, Reggie's three dingers in a single '77 Series game. The House that Ruth Built. The asymmetrical horseshoe on East 161st Street and River Avenue in the Bronx, New York.

Yankee Stadium!

As Damon saunters up to the plate, Seth is wondering why Papa Sol didn't tell anyone at the birthday party yesterday he was going to be here tonight. Maybe he was given only one ticket by a friend and he couldn't *not* go and he didn't want to hurt anyone's feelings? Yeah, that must be it.

And I'll be right there with 'em, you can bet your sweet bippee.

The deep, baritone voice of the great Bob Sheppard, the PA announcer since '51, intones: "Your attention please, ladies and gentlemen. Now batting for the Red Sox, the center fielder, Johnny Damon . . . number eighteen."

Seth's never been here before and, in awe, scans the stadium. There's the famous white-arched facade in the outfield and the short right-field porch and Death Valley in left-center and the "batter's eye," those black-painted seats in dead center.

He looks to his right, at Papa Sol, sees the hope in his eyes because his beloved Red Sox are on the verge of making it back to the Series for the first time since the Buckner Fiasco in '86. Then he sees the disdain in Sol's eyes when he surveys the Yanks settling in on defense, these damn Yankees.

The feeling is multiplied by about a trillion as Sol watches the especially odious Bucky Dent, author of Boston misery in the '78 AL East division playoffs, throw out the first ball. The harbinger of yet another Red Sox postseason disappointment?

The Sox are fortunate to be here. Down 0–3 in the Series, they've scratched and clawed their way back, thanks to a David Ortiz walk-off homer in Game 4, an Ortiz walk-off single in Game 5, and a courageous performance by pitcher Curt Schilling that sent his blood-soaked sock right to Cooperstown. In fact, never has a team come back from being behind three games to none to win a baseball pennant series, and there is tension in the brisk October New York air. Oh, how these Yankees fans hate to lose.

Damon strides up to the dish. The spunky center fielder is only 3-for-29 in the Series so far, but he's hanging in there and strokes a single to left.

Seth looks around him and thinks about what, compared to the others he's been back to visit, is different at this twenty-first-century ball game. What strikes him is the "technology of spectation"—the ubiquity of BlackBerries and cell phones and iPods and electronic hand warmers. All the beeps and rings and musical riffs that punctuate the pauses in the action. A far cry from the fifties, when the most technological device at the ballpark was a hearing aid. Yet the essence of baseball and the fever of the fan have never changed through, and despite, all these advances: The fascination of the game itself and the passion of rooting are every bit as engaging and energizing as they were in '51.

Before you can say David Américo Ortiz, the Bosox grab a quick 2–0 lead in the first, courtesy of the Dominican slugger's two-run blast.

The Yanks go quietly in the bottom of the first, and before Yankees fans can catch their collective breath, the bases are full of Sox in the top of the second, and Damon, on a roll, smashes reliever Javier Vázquez's first offering over the short right-field porch for a grand salami, and Boston is now up 6–0.

What goes around comes around, historian Seth Stein thinks, noting that the Yankees themselves were ahead 6–0 after three innings in Game 1.

Seth is also thinking about why he is here, at this game, at this time. Surely not for the excitement, although Papa Sol and the other Boston fans are plenty excited to see the rout taking place. But Seth already knows the outcome— the Bosox will crush the Bombers in a walk, 10–3—and that the game will be as excitingly close as Secretariat's winning the '73 Belmont by thirty-one lengths.

The other three games he has visited so far were wildly exciting one-run affairs: 5–4 in '51, 1–0 in '62, and 6–5 in '86. So why is he at this one?

What pops into Seth's mind is that during the other three games, Papa Sol was involved in a life-altering act that either affected the actual outcome of the game or was a consequence of it. And since the result of this game will never be in doubt, the only answer can be that yesterday was the last day Papa Sol was seen, so maybe something happened here that resulted in his disappearance from the face of the earth. Something that *just happened to escape the notice of 56,128 witnesses?*

"Papa Sol, please be careful! Don't let anything happen to you!" Seth pleads out of love and concern.

As expected, the plea goes unrequited.

The rest of the game creeps along slow as a sloth for Seth, who knows the outcome of the contest, but not his grandfather's fate.

Damon homers again, and again it is on Vázquez's first pitch (didn't he learn anything from the first time?), and it's 8–1, and then it's 8–3, and then 9–3, then 10–3, and now it's the bottom of the ninth, and with two outs and Lofton on first and Williams on second, Ruben Sierra, pinch-hitting for Olerud, taps a slow roller on a 1-0 pitch to Pokey Reese at second, who tosses the ball to Doug Mientkiewicz at first, and the beloved Red Sox have done it, they've come back from three games to none to knock off those damn Yankees!

Seth is looking at Papa Sol now and remembering all the odd, sad, terrible, fear-inspiring, despairing looks he has seen before in his baseball fanatic grandfather's eyes, but this time, there is no oddness, no sadness, no despair. No, this time there is unbridled joy and gratefulness and unspeakable satisfaction, Papa Sol's eyes reveling in the fact that his Red Sox have just defeated the Yankees, beaten them in grand style, and now they'll be going off to the World Series for the first time in eighteen years, since the Billy B. Affair, and maybe now they'll win their first World Championship since 1918 and these eyes that have seen so much disappointment have now seen much of that disappointment melt away: the failures of Red Sox past, the coming up short of Teddy Ballgame and Pesky and Doerr and Dom, of Lonborg and Yaz and Rico, of Fisk and Rice and, yes, Billy Buckner.

By now, most of the other fans—exhausted either from joy or sorrow—have staggered to the exits and filed out of the Stadium. Sol and Seth are alone, here in their third-baseline seats, here in the stillness of the aftermath. Seth is so happy that Sol is so happy, but still, he wonders, why is he here? Simply to see the joy in his grandfather's face?

And the other fans have now all departed, and noble old Yankee Stadium is host not to 56,129, but to two.

No, wait . . . make that three. Way over there, way down the foul line and making his way toward Papa Sol and his invisible grandson, his faint but piercing whistling filling up the empty ballpark, is a short, distinguished-looking African-American gentleman, in his late sixties perhaps, an employee of the Yankees, and he's sweeping up the aisles with the care and punctiliousness of a brain surgeon.

His progress toward the two baseball fanatics is methodical, and as Seth watches him sweep up the aisles and wend his way over toward him and his grandfather, he does not notice what Papa Sol is doing.

Papa Sol, an angelic grin still adorning his face, is falling over, falling straight ahead and to his right, his body landing with a dull thud halfway into the aisle, his head thwacking against the concrete, his eyes closed by the impact.

Seth does not notice this turn of events, his attention still riveted on the black gentleman who, to his left, is lovingly cleaning up the detritus left by the untidy fans and who is still wending his way toward the two Steins.

And now Seth looks to his right and sees that Papa Sol is lying there halfway in the aisle and tries to pick him up but of course he can't and *omygod* is this the way it all ends? and the joy and the peace and the satisfaction inside of Seth have turned into fear and panic and helplessness.

Sol, still stunned, comes to and struggles to his seat and gazes straight ahead at the playing field, an odd, vacant look on his face and clearly in some sort of daze.

Seth sits there, wide-eyed and terrified, wondering what will happen to Papa Sol now? and is he in any pain? and here comes that gentleman, that neurosurgeon of ballpark sweepers, who is sweeping up a pile of debris a few rows down. Seth notices that under a box of half-eaten popcorn and a paper cup with a few inches of beer still in it, hidden by this debris, is a square brown leather object, and it's Papa Sol's wallet, which must've fallen down there when Sol fell up here. And the whistling sweeper sweeps the wallet into his bin just like that, oblivious to inaudible Seth's begging him not to.

The sweeper looks up and sees dazed Solomon Stein, who sits in his state of apparent oblivion, staring vacantly out at the empty playing field, the field that just a brief while ago had been the source of his unbridled and quite lucid happiness.

"Hey, man, you okay?" the sweeper asks.

Nothing.

"Hey, mister, you okay?"

Like Seth, Papa Sol seems to be in a faraway place, one removed from his accustomed present.

The sweeper takes Sol by the shoulder and shakes him. "Hey, mister—"

"Huh?"

"You okay?"

"Oh, I guess so. Who are you?" Sol asks.

"Name's Walter. Walter Retlaw. But my friends call me Wally."

"Well, then I'll call you Wally. How ya doing, Wally?"

"I'm doing just fine. Question is, how *you* doing?"

"I'm doing pretty good, Wally. I guess . . ."

Wally the sweeper notices a trickle of blood dripping down Sol's forehead, dripping from a nasty, swollen little bruise.

"We better take care of this," Wally says, pointing to Sol's abrasion. "What's your name, and where do you live?"

"Um, I'm not sure. Um . . ."

Uh-oh, something is wrong, Seth thinks, powerless to help out.

"Well, now, do you have a wallet?"

Papa Sol pats down both pants pockets, then his back pockets, then his jacket pockets.

"Nope, guess I don't have one."

"Listen, I better take you home and clean up that wound. First-aid station's closed, but my place isn't too far from here. Not to worry, everything will straighten itself out in the end, my friend, you'll see," Wally says reassuringly.

And Wally the sweeper and still-dazed Papa Sol and invisible Seth walk slowly out of the stadium, out into the quiet, chilly streets of the Bronx. . .

⚾

. . . and up to Wally Retlaw's apartment building.

Seth makes a mental note of the address on the Grand Concourse as he follows Papa Sol and his host up the narrow staircase. When they get to the third floor, Wally puts the key in the door of apartment number 303, welcomes his guest, and closes the door just after his uninvited, invisible second guest sneaks in.

Wally's digs are a lot like him: small, modest, understated, uncomplicated. In fact, a writer desiring to describe its contents would probably have a pretty easy job of it.

In the bedroom, there's a small bed with a handsome blue plaid comforter and an end table, on top of which sit a silver-and-black alarm clock radio and a slender, elegant black desk lamp.

The kitchen sports a simple gas stove and a small, round table flanked by two stylish bridge chairs.

In the living room: a rust-colored mohair sofa, a kidney-shaped glass coffee table punctuated by a vase of fresh red roses, an entertainment center with TV and stereo, and a painted black bookcase holding fifty or so volumes, mostly old tomes about the history of baseball. On the wall above the sofa, Wally's past and passion are reflected in three handsomely framed photos of old Negro League baseball stars: Josh Gibson, Satchel Paige, and Cool Papa Bell.

"Sit yourself down, young man," Wally Retlaw says, with a kindly wink. "Can I get you anything to drink? Cup of java? Bottled water? Ginger ale? Maybe even a little Canadian Club?"

Sol shakes his head.

"Well then, let's take a look at that bruise."

Wally excuses himself for a second and returns with a hand towel, a bottle of peroxide, a tube of Neosporin, and a Band-Aid. He cleans up the dried blood and dabs the bruise on Sol's forehead and applies the Band-Aid and the antibiotic ointment with precision and caring.

"There, that should do it," Wally says. "Oh, like I told you, my name is Wally Retlaw. I'm seventy-five. Been living here in this beautiful mansion for ten years now, ever since my darling Louise passed on. So what happened to your head, my friend?"

Sol thinks a moment. "Don't really know. Think I bumped it. Maybe fell down."

Seth notes that Papa Sol's speech is slow and unsure. Something is definitely not kosher.

"Looks like you enjoy baseball," Wally says. "That's something we share, for sure. Been a huge part of my own life. Yessir, I've followed it, oh, maybe since I was six. Seen 'em all come through the Stadium: Ruth, Gehrig, Lazzeri, Meusel, Dickey, DiMaggio, Rizzuto, Mantle, Berra, Ford, Reggie, Munson, Jeter."

Papa Sol looks with amiable vacancy at his new acquaintance.

"But my favorites were the old Negro League ballplayers. Guys like Cool Papa Bell, Satch, Gibson, the two Bucks, Judy Johnson, Ray Dandridge. Seen many of 'em play, I did. Also saw, or else heard about, a lot of the old teams. Homestead Grays, Pittsburgh Crawfords, K.C. Monarchs, Baltimore Elite Giants, not to mention the likes of the Atlanta Black Crackers, the Chattanooga Black Lookouts, the Denver White Elephants, the Ethiopian Clowns, the St. Paul

Colored Gophers, the Zulu Cannibal Giants, and, last but not least, the Waggoner Greasing Palaces Baseball Club."

Wally chuckles a deep bass chuckle that fills the entire apartment.

"Yup, I sure do love this ol' game," Wally continues. "For most of my professional life, I ran a small baseball business, yes indeedy. Cards, uniforms, balls, memorabilia, that kind of thing. Did pretty well for myself, if I must say. Retired when Louise passed, but I couldn't stay away from the game. No way. So I got this gig at the Stadium a few years back. It wasn't for money, it was for love. A second life, you might say. I adore the job. Gets me out, and back to the park that's meant so much to me. Eighty-one days a year, don't you know. The fans are great, and so's the management. Even met Steinbrenner once. Nice guy."

Papa Sol remains speechless.

"So, what'd you think of the game tonight? You a Yankees fan?"

"Um, I think the game was good. Don't really recall all the details, but I had a nice time. Am I a Yankees fan? Well, yeah, I guess so."

Something is wrong, Seth is thinking. *Terribly* wrong.

"You haven't told me what your name was," Wally says.

"Um . . . er . . . it's . . . it's . . ."

Seth Stein can't bear to watch and closes his eyes.

⚾

Seth Stein opens his eyes. He is slouching in his La-Z-Boy in his Cambridge town house, arms at his sides. On the arm of the chair, in its ashtray, his Cohiba Esplendidos reclines, still lit, a thin wisp of smoke snaking its way toward the ceiling.

Holy moley.

Seth's brain is teeming with questions. What actually happened to Papa Sol? Was it amnesia? Was he in any pain? Will he be all right? Is he . . . *still alive?* Did he ever snap out of it? Did he end up staying these past two years with Wally? And yet: Did all this *really* happen? Part of Seth wants to rush out this instant and jump in Jezebel and drive down to the Bronx and rescue his Papa Sol. The other part wants to scream what are you, a crazy lunatic?

Seth is emotionally spent and doesn't have a drop of gas left in the tank. Amid all the worrying and concern, he is solaced by a single image: the sight of Papa Sol and Wally Retlaw together in the modest Bronx apartment. How touching was Wally's concern for Sol's well-being. What sweetness and compassion he showed. And, like Papa Sol, he was a baseball fanatic, so even if Sol didn't regain his memory, they could still share this passion. *That is, if all this really happened . . .*

There's one thing that's still bugging Seth, though, and he picks up the phone.

"Gordon? Yeah, I know it's late, but I've got a really important question for you. Shouldn't take long. Basically, the writing's going well, but I've hit a snag. One of the historical figures I'm exploring in the opening chapter had an accident in the latter part of his life. Fell down and bumped his head. Seems like after that, he didn't remember things, important things, like his name, what happened in the past. It sounds to me like amnesia, but I know virtually nothing about it, so can you give me a quick diagnosis?"

"Listen, Seth," Gordon Stewart answers, "this is pretty hard to do over the phone. But if you need a quick fix, I need to know a few things."

"Shoot."

"Well, how old was this guy? And what kind of bump are we talking about?"

"He was, I dunno, maybe in his sixties, seventies. Unfortunately, there's not much biographical information available. According to the few medical records I found, it wasn't a huge bump, but it did break the skin and was a little swollen and bloody."

"Hmmm. Listen, Seth, don't hold me to this, but my best guess is that yes, it does sound a lot like amnesia to me. Actually, it's called retrograde amnesia. In older people, this can certainly result from an episode of what we call a TIA, or transient ischemic attack, a common event, a ministroke really, which might be brought on by a heightened emotional state. Before the fall, do you know if the guy was really happy or really despondent about anything?"

"It happened after an important, historic . . . political victory, so yes, he must've been really happy—"

"That makes sense. So he might've had this TIA, and it might've produced an overload of epinephrine in his body. This might then have caused him to fall over, and the bump on his head might've resulted in the retrograde amnesia, which means that you forget virtually everything in your life that preceded the bump. Technically speaking, the head trauma affects the hippocampus, which is responsible for long-term memory, and/or the inferior aspects of the temporal lobe, which play a role in the memory of both visual and auditory events."

"Whoa! That's plenty, Gordon! My left brain is on overload! But thanks so much for your knowledge and expertise. It all makes sense to me."

"No problemo, my friend. Now don't quote me on any of this, but as far as I can tell, this guy almost certainly had retrograde amnesia."

"One last question, Gordon. It's not clear what happened to him after the accident, but out of curiosity, do people generally snap out of it?"

"That's impossible to say. Sometimes they do, and sometimes they don't. All depends on the severity of the trauma, and on how much brain matter was affected by the blow. I'm afraid I'm not smart enough to help you there."

"Thanks again, Gordon. I'll let you go now. See you for coffee in the morning."

Seth can hardly keep his eyes open, but a final thought filters through his brain: Let History record that Papa Sol's life may have been filled with bumps and frustrations and major disappointments and burst dream bubbles and self-doubt, but in the end, it was a good life, and who knows?, maybe it's still a life that's being lived and enjoyed at some level. So maybe he never got to savor the fact that his beloved Bosox finally won the Series. But even if he never got back his memory, maybe he enjoyed the rest of his time on this earth. And whether he did or not, I'll always have the memories of him and his love inside me.

Seth draws on his Cohiba, tightens his lips in the shape of a lowercase *o,* and snaps both jaws toward each other, but only halfway together. Out of his mouth springs the most elegant smoke ring he has ever fabricated. It is round and paper-thin. It has no jagged edges or wobbles. It retains the precise form with which it was born as it wafts its way heavenward. It seems like it will keep on floating upward forever.

It is perfection.

Seth admires his creation a while, closes the top of the wooden box holding the baseball, then a cartoon lightbulb appears above his head in a thought balloon. There is something pressing he has to do first thing in the morning, something that can wait no longer.

⚾

Doddering, dependable Jezebel sputters up the crack-filled, grass-sprouted driveway and parks her big butt there, sweating the usual droplets of oil on the pavement.

Seth bounds out of her, gives her the requisite, affectionate pat on the roof, unlocks the door of the grizzled, grey-shingled house of Elsie Adler Stein, ascends the thirteen creaking stairs.

"Honey, I'm home!"

Seated at her dressing table, a beaming, spry Grandma Elfie greets her grandson with a warm embrace. Today, she is no longer the bedraggled Eve from the Masaccio fresco, but one of the smiling, vivacious ladies in the foreground of Renoir's *Le Moulin de la Galette*.

"Gram," Seth says, his voice trembling with excitement, "I've got something really important to tell you that you're not gonna believe. Are you ready?"

6

SETHAROO

ELSIE NODS.

"Well," Seth says, "for starters—"

"I love you, Setharoo!"

Seth's eyes cloud up, because the nickname is one that only Papa Sol had ever used. He is happy to hear the words come out of his grandmother's mouth now. And such words.

"Gram, I'm going to tell you a story . . ."

Elsie smiles her radiant smile. She loves it when Seth tells her stories, just like his Papa Sol used to tell stories to him.

". . . and the name of the story is 'The Secrets of Solomon Stein.' "

Elsie smiles again, even more broadly. Seth pauses, wipes his eyes, begins his tale.

He tells her of the beautiful hand-carved Solomon Stein wooden box and the scuffed baseball and the spinning room and the Fantastical Historical Slide Show.

Elsie opens her eyes wide.

He speaks of the trip to 1951 and walking around Borough Park and the cars and the smells and the shoes and the songs.

Elsie's eyes twinkle.

He relates his tour of 1270 and Papa Sol chiseling in the basement and Elsie and Sol watching Uncle Miltie in bed and guffawing like crazy lunatics.

Elsie giggles.

He recounts the story of the Polo Grounds and the Game and the Catch and Papa Sol's intensity.

Elsie's mouth opens.

He narrates the scene in the basement with the pistol to the temple and the look in Papa Sol's eyes.

Elsie's mouth opens wider.

He reports the discoveries of the ticket stub and the mustard stain.

Elsie nods approval.

He regales her with the trip to 1962 and the scene in Berkeley and Papa Sol and fourteen-year-old Simon playing that game where Simon imitates the different players.

Elsie titters.

He describes the game at Candlestick and the empty stare on Sol's face as he read the article in the *Chronicle* the next morning.

Elsie frowns.

He gives an account of the sunburn in the mirror and the trip to 1986 and Sol telling Seth the story of "The Curse of the Bambino" in Cambridge and the look of love in Sol's eyes.

Elsie sheds a tear.

He chronicles the story of Shea and the Mets and the Bosox and sitting next to Janet and Nathan Detroit and Sol's fervor and his shouting at Buckner and the ball oozing between BB's legs and watching Papa Sol cry for the very first time.

Elsie sheds a second tear.

He talks about the trip to 2004 and how happy Papa Sol was when the beloved Red Sox beat the damn Yankees in Game 7 of the ALCS.

Elsie grins.

He conveys to her the story of Papa Sol falling down and bumping his head and then how Wally the sweeper was so kind to him and took him home to his apartment and cleaned up the wound and talked to Papa Sol about his passion for baseball and how even though Papa Sol didn't remember very much, he seemed to be perfectly happy to be together with Wally.

Elsie frowns, then her face breaks out in a gorgeous smile.

"That was such a lovely story, *bubeleh*," Elsie says. "You've always had such a vivid imagination!"

Seth is dying to tell her that maybe it's not make-believe and maybe it all really happened and maybe someday they'll both see Papa Sol again. But until he's certain, he will leave it at that, a lovely story that has made his Grandma Elfie happy.

Elsie is suddenly tired, but the fatigue is pleasant and profound. She walks to the bed and puts her beautiful, weary head on the soft pillow.

"By the way, Grandma, who was Janet? And the guy with the scar on his face?"

Elsie is too tired to wonder how Seth knew about Janet and Scarface.

"Her name is Janet Zwerdling, my sweet . . . your surrogate mother . . . real mother unable to conceive . . . Papa Sol kept in touch after your parents died . . . paid them back . . . guy with scar is husband, Doug . . . Papa Sol and I agreed . . . better if you didn't know, *dahlink* . . . less complicated . . . and your mother, the wife of your father, loved you so . . ."

Now it is Seth's mouth that is wide open.

This explains why he never saw any resemblance between himself and the photo of his mother. This explains the bulging envelope at Shea.

"I love you, Elsie Stein," he says, holding back tears.

"I love you, Seth Stein," she answers, scrunching her nose.

Grandma Elsie clasps her hands together on her belly. She is tired but still radiant. Her eyes have stopped twinkling, her mouth has closed, her nods and giggles and frowns and titters and grins have ceased, her tears have dried.

Nothing remains on her face but a regal aura of peace and tranquility and serenity and satisfaction and love, just like in one of those diaphanous and breathlessly gorgeous cinematic scenes featuring Greer Garson or Loretta Young.

Seth looks at her with love and compassion. What she must have gone through these past two years. He turns his head toward the dressing table, stares at the sepia Lake George photo of Papa Sol and Grandma Elsie and the black-and-white photo of his parents and the color photo of Papa Sol and Willie Mays. His eyes find Gram again and she seems so happy now and she has fallen into a totally peaceful sleep for the first time in two years.

And for the first time in his entire adult life, as he looks at his happy and peaceful Grandma Elsie, Seth loses it. He is bawling like a baby and the tears are chubby and strong and keep coming and don't want to stop and they are flowing out of both eyes and splashing onto his jeans and he doesn't give a damn and it feels oh so good.

The tears stop at last, and Seth leans over and plants a tender kiss on Grandma Elsie's forehead.

◖◗

Seth is reclining in his La-Z-Boy, Balvenie, rocks, twist, half splash in hand.

His eyes wander to Papa Sol's wooden box, there on the table. He gets up, brings it back to the chair, places it on his lap, opens it, and beholds the old, scuffed Bobby Thomson baseball. This time, he will just look at it.

He is thinking about his extraordinary trips to the past that no other nonfiction human being has ever been privileged to take and how they revealed to him not only Papa Sol's secrets, but also his flaws, his idealism and his broken dreams, his concerns and his fears, his passion and his empathy. He is thinking about the mysteries in Papa Sol's life that no one ever knew about and also about Mark Twain's quote "History never repeats itself; at best it sometimes rhymes," and how odd it is that *history* and *mystery* share their rhyme with no other word in the English language, and did the mischievous Twain mean to suggest that?

He is thinking about these privileged trips and about History and can we ever know it? Is History after all, as Schopenhauer and Churchill and Whitman thought, an imperfect and flawed discipline? About the historian's dilemma of patching together the quilt of bygone events. About the inevitable evanescence of time. About the passion of former days. About the daunting challenge of finding the real truth concerning what happened *then*.

He is thinking about how this particular baseball is not only a baseball, but a metaphor for knowledge—just like the game of baseball is a metaphor for something deeper and more visceral—and how it has made him a happier and a fuller person. About what the game of baseball has to teach about the human condition, how it has compelled him to rededicate himself to studying History with a new freshness, a new sense of an open mind, a new wisdom and insight, and how what is important is not the baseball itself—this inanimate object made of horsehide and with the 108 crimson stitches holding it together—but rather the history of his grandfather's life, which he now harbors inside himself and which this old scuffed ball has allowed him to feel, right here, *in his nerves and vitals.*

He is thinking about how amazing it is that as a student and scholar of the traditionally vicarious discipline of History, he has now become part of it and were his visits to the past really real or just dreams but what about the stub and the stain and the sunburn and the Mets cap?

Seth closes the wooden box, gets up, stretches, starts removing his clothes. Shower time.

The steaming sprays splash pingily off Seth's back. He moans with pleasure as the fingers of water massage his skin, soften his tense muscles—deltoid, erector spinae, intertransversarii, latissimus dorsi, levator scapulae, rhomboid major and minor, supraspinatus, teres major and minor, trapezius.

He closes his eyes, allows his weary mind to meander. It is wandering to the brilliant words and music of Gilbert and Sullivan, recalling all the songs Papa Sol used to teach him, the melodies he used to listen to through the years. From *Iolanthe, The Mikado, The Yeoman of the Guard, Pirates, Pinafore, Patience, The Gondoliers.*

In a contemplative fashion,
And a tranquil frame of mind,
Free from every kind of passion,
Some solution let us find.
Let us grasp the situation,
Solve the complicated plot,
Quiet, calm deliberation
Disentangles every knot.

Disentangles every knot.

Disentangles every knot—

Leapin' lizards.

Seth's eyes open wide. He has just had one of his epiphanies. It has come out of nowhere, as frequently happens in the shower. No rhyme, no reason, just the way his quirky brain works, a creative miracle, an irrational fluke, a random stroke of genius.

The lyrics have somehow reminded him of that cryptic note Papa Sol left him, the one he has yet to decode, perhaps the final piece of the puzzle? For some reason, the throwaway line in the note just popped into his head in the shower, *bling!,* just like that.

That is all you need to know.

Of course!

Seth turns off the water, dries himself, throws on his Harvard T and jeans, sprints to his study. He takes Papa Sol's note out of the top drawer of his desk, rummages through a few piles of books strewn on the floor. There it is, there, the little leather-bound anthology of Romantic poems Sol and Elfie gave him twenty years ago for his Bar Mitzvah.

He sits down at his desk, opens the book up to a poem, places the opened book side by side with the note:

"Beauty is truth, truth beauty,"—that is all
Ye know on earth, and all ye need to know."

That is all you need to know.

Yikes.

This is no throwaway line. It is the key that will unlock the note's door.

The poem is John Keats's "Ode on a Grecian Urn." Papa Sol loved it, Seth recalls, loved the Greekness of it, the mythology, even read it to him once or twice. He also remembers having read it in high school. Now, as he makes his way through the poem, deep in exegetical meditation, it all comes flooding back to him, as mystery cedes to meaning.

> *Thou still unravish'd bride of quietness,*
>   *Thou foster-child of Silence and slow Time,*
> *Sylvan historian . . .*

Sylvan historian! Seth looks at Papa Sol's note, sitting on the desk, to the right of the poem:

My dearest Sylvan one.

Yesss. The Grecian urn, subject of the poem, is addressed by the poet as a "sylvan historian," since one of the scenes it relates on its surface has a woodsy setting. And yes, I, Seth Stein, just like the urn, am a historian, too, a "Sylvan one." So far, so good.

Seth reads the remainder of the first stanza, and his eyes drift down to the beginning of the second:

> *Heard melodies are sweet, but those unheard*
>   *Are sweeter; therefore, ye soft pipes, play on;*
> *Not to the sensual ear, but, more endear'd,*
>   *Pipe to the spirit ditties of no tone . . .*

Ditties of no tone! And now to Papa Sol's note:

My spirit hears nothing if not ditties of no tone.

So. The urn, or art, can capture "unheard melodies," which are sweeter than ones we hear in real life. Papa Sol was a human being but also a sensitive artist. He understood about the music no one can hear except those whose spirits can appreciate the idealized melodies that are art and that, unlike reality, are toneless and eternal. And Papa Sol was a Romantic, a dreamer with a lofty spirit.

Now to the second part of the third stanza:

> *More happy love! more happy, happy love!*
>   *For ever warm and still to be enjoy'd,*
>   *For ever panting, and for ever young;*
> *All breathing human passion far above,*
>   *That leaves a heart high-sorrowful and cloy'd,*
>   *A burning forehead, and a parching tongue . . .*

A burning forehead, and a parching tongue! And Sol:

> *My forehead burns, my tongue is parched.*

Okay. The amorous scene depicted on the urn is one of lovers frozen in time, eternal passions frozen by art that will last forever. Only problem here is that the passion is idealized, frozen by art, and can never be consummated. In the note, Papa Sol implied that his human passion was also "far above," ideal, unsatisfied. Like the lovers, his passion was often unfulfilled. Must have been referring to the Ball and the Terry Fiasco and the Billy Blunder and maybe other disappointments? This must have been how he saw his life: passionate, but also, in part, disappointing and incomplete.

Now on to stanza four, and the final three verses:

And, little town, thy streets for evermore
  Will silent be; and not a soul, to tell
    Why thou art desolate, can e'er return . . .

And Sol's version:

Can a soul ever return from the silent streets of a little town?

Wow. So, the town pictured on the urn is empty, and the poet is saying that it will always be empty, since art has frozen it in time. But also, no one from the past, from the time when the streets of the town were empty, can ever come back to life to explain why there were no people there.

History! Of course. Papa Sol must have been thinking of me, his Sylvan historian, when he wrote this. The people of the past have disappeared forever and can't return to life, so it is up to the historian to go back and answer the questions.

It is up to the historian to go back and answer the questions.

Go back: as a scholar, as a researcher, or . . . *literally?*

If I'd gone back to the Polo Grounds and Candlestick and Shea and Yankee Stadium as an ordinary historian, via my research, I would've put some of the pieces of the past together, but, of course, not nearly all of them, since History is an imperfect discipline, as I've learned from Whitehead and Churchill and others.

But I might have gone back . . . *literally.* Ridiculous as it seems, could Papa Sol have known, as reflected in his note, that the baseball he bequeathed to me would actually take me back to the frozen past, then allow me to return to the present to tell about it? Could he possibly have known that it would permit me to go back and see him as he really was, warts and all?

Seth is flushed with the power of discovery, of knowledge, of clarification, of an even deeper love for his Papa Sol. He presses on, and now he is reading the first line of the fifth and final stanza:

O Attic shape! . . .

And Sol:

Your legacy is in the Attic.

Aha. So I was right to assume the capital *A* had to do with the Greeks, not something buried in Grandma Elsie's attic. Of course, and now I see: The essence of what he wanted to give to me in life resides in the Greeks, in their heroism and their high ideals and their art. In the end, life is flawed by its imperfections, so you have to hold fast to high ideals and dreams, and reach for something lofty.

Seth inserts the note in the book, on the same page as the Keats poem. And he grins a crooked grin: Papa Sol's note—the perfect, clarifying companion to the magical baseball—is no longer Greek to him.

⚾

Seth is sitting in his office in Robinson Hall, which exhibits the same studied chaos as in his town house: Baseball memorabilia, history tomes, and random note cards and paper are arranged haphazardly and in such a way that, aside from Seth, no human being could ever find anything, or even want to.

The Brahms Horn Trio is playing on the iTunes of his

Apple laptop. Seth always listens to Brahms when he is trying to organize his thoughts.

He is putting the final touches on his outline for the
second chapter of his book, and he is stuck. Whenever
Seth hits a brick wall, he grabs a pen and a pad and starts
scribbling words. Any words that come to mind. Spontaneous, random lists of words. And invariably, by dint of
this creative, cathartic, and free-flowing process, he extri-
cates himself out of the quicksand of writer's block.

He writes his name first, and then Kate's, Elsie's, and
Sammy's. Followed by lists of sea mammals, baseball man-
agers under fifty, U.S. presidents with long beards, symphonies beginning with the letter *C,* curly Italian pasta,
African capitals, Chilean vineyards, sculptures by Michelangelo, novels by Dickens, makes of acoustic guitars.

Another page of the writing pad. He jots down Papa
Sol's name, and his mind wanders back to his four visits,
and he scribbles some more names, right under Sol's:

Solomon Stein
Bobby Thomson
San Francisco
Billy Buckner
Walter Retlaw

Something about this particular list catches his eye. Not
sure what, but it's definitely something. He reads the
names first silently, then aloud. Nope, nothing jumps out at
him except for the alliterations in Solomon Stein and Billy
Buckner. Then what in the world—

Suffering sciatica.

Like a prehistoric termite trapped in a tomb of amber,
Seth is frozen stiff by his discovery. He counts once again,

just to be sure. Yup, every single name he has just listed, every single one of the entities that played major roles in his four visits to the past, contains *precisely twelve letters*.

Someone with a mind less agile and persistent than Seth's might have dismissed this as a meaningless coincidence. Seth Stein, on the other hand, will not be satisfied until he has exhausted all roads to the truth.

After all, VERITAS.

He Googles on his iBook G4, types in *twelve,* clicks on SEARCH.

Mother of pearl.

The basic sales unit in trade is twelve, or a dozen.
The Western and Chinese zodiacs have twelve signs.
There are twelve heavenly bodies in our Solar System.
There are twelve months in a year.
There are twelve hours in half a day, and twelve numbers on a clock.
The basic units of time (60 seconds, 60 minutes, 24 hours) can all perfectly divide by twelve.
The minute hand of a clock turns twelve times as fast as the hour hand.
Jewish tradition talks of the twelve tribes of Israel.
The New Testament describes twelve apostles of Jesus.
In traditional Jewish practice, a girl becomes a bat mitzvah on her twelfth birthday.
There are twelve days of Christmas.
In Greek mythology, the Twelve Olympians were the principal gods of the pantheon.
In Greek mythology, Hercules was assigned Twelve Labors.
In English, twelve is the largest number that has just one syllable.

In the U.S., twelve people are appointed to sit on a jury.
There are twelve pairs of ribs in the human body.
There are twelve major joints in the human body.

Okay, so the number twelve is an amazing, incredible, international, universal, essential, significant, mystical, omnipotent number. So what? The real question: What are the names of the highlights from his visits trying to convey to him?

Seth takes another look at one of his Google links. And there it is, in the etymology of the word *twelve*:

> The word "twelve" is a native English word that presumably arises from the Germanic compound *twa-lif,* "two-leave," meaning that two is left after one takes away the base, ten . . . so a literal translation would yield "two remaining [after having ten taken]."

Two remaining after having ten taken. Seth scratches his head, thinks hard.

And sees the light.

①

Battered brown leather briefcase in hand, Seth Stein scurries through the Yard—Weld, University, Thayer—then passes Annenberg Hall and heads up Oxford. His mind is racing almost as quickly as his feet, but stopping his momentum cold is a disheveled, scholarly-looking homeless person.

"Spare a buck for a cup of coffee?"

Although Seth is in a rush, he is feeling magnanimous, so he reaches into his jeans pocket, fumbles, pulls out a not-so-crisp dollar bill, gives it to his new friend, with a smile and a "good luck, man."

Whatever happened to "Buddy, can you spare a *dime*?", Seth wonders.

As he continues up Oxford Street, his feet screech to a halt. What was that I felt there in my pocket, next to the bill?

He fumbles around in the pocket again, does his "blind man palpating" guessing game with his right hand. Can't quite tell what that object is. He removes it from his pocket, walks closer to a light coming from a nearby building so he can get a better look.

The object is a pair of peanuts in their shell, the kind he rarely eats, the kind you can find at a baseball game.

Mamma mia.

A stunned Seth is standing outside the door of Kate's apartment. He is thinking about this latest piece of prima facie evidence. He is thinking that the camel's back is now officially broken by the straw that is the ballpark peanuts. As if the ticket stub, the mustard stain, the sunburn, and the Mets cap weren't enough to make him a true believer.

But he is mostly thinking about the number *twelve* and its etymology.

Two remaining after having ten taken.

He is reviewing in his mind his original conclusion about the significance of this sentence. *Two remaining after having ten taken.* Ten taken. First my folks died in a plane crash. That's two. Then Kate's maternal grandparents died in a car crash. That's four. Then her father's parents passed around the same time, of natural causes. That's six. Then Kate's parents died in that horrendous elevator accident. That's eight. And Papa Sol disappeared, and when he did, a big chunk of Gram's life was taken away. That's ten. I never knew my mother's parents, so it's still ten. And so they've all been taken, these family members of mine and Kate's, the ten of them. And now there are two remaining.

"Hey, babe, willya grab me that bottle of Barolo?" Seth tells Kate as he sweeps her off her feet, pulls her back nearly to the floor, and plants a passionate smackeroo on her lips, reproducing that V-J Day photo on the cover of *Life*.

"Wow, lover boy!" Kate purrs. "What'd I do to deserve *that*?"

"You'll see," Seth reassures her. "But first," he adds in his best Gabby Hayes twang, "this here goldarn varmint of a bottle needs t'be opened, an' *right quick*."

While Seth opens the wine, Kate is wondering why the Barolo? She knows that Seth knows that she's been saving it for a very special occasion, so—

"Sweetie," Seth says, wineglass in hand, "sit your cute rump down. I've got something to tell you I've been wanting to tell you for a while now."

Knowing better than to get her hopes up, Kate registers a look of apprehension.

"No, it's nothing bad, dear. It's all good."

Seth and Kate sip, and he proceeds to tell her the story—the entire story, in exquisite detail and five-part harmony—of his four amazing visits to Papa Sol and the past, including every bit of prima facie evidence. It requires a full hour to tell her everything, to open up his mind and his heart and his soul.

He is finished now, spent physically and emotionally. He takes a second sip of the precious wine and leans against the back of the sofa.

Kate is exhausted, too. She has spent the entire sixty minutes, literally and figuratively, on the edge of her seat.

Smiling. Frowning. Giggling. Laughing. Crying. Cheering. Booing. Getting angry. Getting happy. Being frightened. Being proud.

"So you believe me? You think it all actually happened?" he asks.

"*Of course,* I believe you," she answers, this time without hesitating. "This kind of thing doesn't happen to just anyone," she continues, "but you're not just anyone. I love you, Seth Stein."

Seth pauses a sec. *Two remaining after having ten taken.*

"I love you, Kate Stein."

Not sure she heard right, Kate has a spasm in the pit of her stomach.

"Se-eth?"

"Yeah?"

She gives him one of those innocent, doe-eyed Lucy Ricardo looks. "What're . . . you . . . saying?"

"What I'm saying, my sweetie pie," Seth says as he raises his glass of the special wine high in the air, "is that . . ."

Seth is thinking about how life is too damn short to put off important things like this anymore and about how proud Papa Sol would be of him at this very moment.

". . . is that . . . *I propose* . . ."

◖◗

The La-Z-Boy is where Seth always ends up when he is feeling anything of any consequence: sadness, happiness, fear, pride, pensiveness, despair, hope. Or ecstasy, which he is feeling now.

Last night was a once-in-a-lifetime evening, and Seth has returned home today from Kate's apartment experiencing an entire gamut of feelings, from Amorousness to the need to stack some *Z*'s.

He is reclining in his La-Z-Boy, smoking the last of his stash of Cohibas to celebrate his engagement to Kate, and his sharing with her the four visits to the past and the rest of his life. He is listening to the original recording of the old Broadway chestnut *Show Boat.* The one recorded opening night, 1927, at the Ziegfeld Theatre.

He blows a series of exquisite little smoke rings that follow one another up to the ceiling like an ethereal string of pearls. The very shape of the ring sequence expresses his inner joy:

o o o o o o o

There's something about a Kern and Hammerstein musical that always makes Seth happy. Here comes one of his favorite songs, one that Papa Sol used to whistle all the time, a real tearjerker actually written by Charles K. Harris in 1892, as performed by the wonderful Frederica von Stade in the role of Magnolia Ravenal:

After the ball is over, after the break of morn,
After the dancers' leaving, after the stars are gone,
Many a heart is aching, if you could read them all—
Many the hopes that have vanished . . . after the ball.

As the final syllable of this quatrain dissolves into the air, Seth projects his head and neck forward jerkily, doing his very finest pigeon imitation.
Thuffering thuccotash.
The final piece of the puzzle. The last line of Papa Sol's note. The passion for word games he and his grandfather share.
P.S. What will you do after the ball?
Seth springs out of his chair, walks to the stereo, replays

the song. Then a third time. Then, one by one, each bar. Then again. And again. Then he returns to his recliner and meditates.

Aha.

After the ball is over. Double entendre. After the dance, this lovely, thrilling dance through time. And also after the baseball has performed its magic, has fulfilled its function as the vehicle for knowledge.

After the break of morn. Another double entendre? When the night has passed and he can see things in the clear light of day. And if the homonym of *morn* is considered—*mourn*—could it also mean after the sadness is gone, the sadness of Papa Sol's disappointments, the sadness of Papa Sol's disappearing? Could he somehow have sensed he was someday going to leave us?

After the dancers' leaving, after the stars are gone. Yet another double meaning. After the visits to the past are over and the stage is empty and morning has broken. But also all the *stars* are gone now. The Dodgers and Giants of the '51 epic are a distant memory. So are the Yankees and Giants of '62. The Bosox and Mets players of '86 are no longer Bosox and Mets. And even from the 2004 ALCS, only a handful of Red Sox and Yanks have remained with their teams.

Many a heart is aching, if you could read them all. There was certainly a bittersweet element in Papa Sol's world. Like the Keats poem, this song is a Romantic piece, and Papa Sol was a Romantic whose ultimate baseball dreams were unfulfilled. But there is sadness for many hearts in this world, too. If I could read them all? Maybe this means me, as historian, making sense of the struggling and suffering of humanity?

Many the hopes that have vanished . . . after the ball. Many of Papa Sol's hopes did vanish. The promise of the Thomson baseball. The dream that the Giants would win the Series again, that the Bosox would win the Series in his lifetime. But now, after the ball has performed its magic, what of my hopes?: *What will you do after the ball?* Well, *my* hopes are still strong. The baseball has given me more clarity about Papa Sol's life and about History itself. And the Bosox *did* win it all in '04, and hope is alive for even more glory. And of course, I have Sammy and Elfie and Kate, and the rest of my life to live.

What will I do after the ball? How will I conduct my life from this point forward? We shall see, Papa Sol, we shall see. . . .

Seth draws in a mouthful of smoke from his Cohiba, expels it in a puffy, gray billow. He is experiencing the relief and the satisfaction of having completely deciphered Sol's note, of having gained access to his secrets.

But *all* of them?

Seth is thinking about how much he has learned, but also about what may be unresolved. Are there still unanswered questions about Papa Sol's life?

He is thinking about how doubt and ignorance are certainty and knowledge's other side of the coin. About whether we can really know another human being. Aren't there always secrets that are left unraveled? Don't Papa Sol's reflect those hidden, unshared pockets of experience harbored by every single human being who ever walked the earth? Don't they reveal a universal truth about life, about its complexity and its unpredictability?

He is thinking about the old quandary that has preoccupied him for such a long time, that is the core question of his teaching and his new book. Is History, in fact, dead as a doornail, as Schopenhauer thought? Or can it be revived?

Shower time.

Seth rests his Cohiba in the ashtray, disrobes, enters the stall. The steamy pinpricks of water put him in a singing mood.

When the red, red robin
comes bob, bob bobbin' . . .
Bob, bob—
Bob, bob—
Shades of Bacchus.

Seth thought he'd had enough epiphanies lately to keep him happy, but apparently, he's not quite through with them. He can't get the *bob, bob* part of the song out of his head, and now he knows why.

Palindrome!

He has always loved the concept of palindromes, those letter clusters or words or sentences that read the same backward and forward. Papa Sol first introduced him to these fascinating linguistic phenomena when he was around seven or eight, and ever since, he has delighted in them, sought new ones out. Started out with simple ones, like the first man's pithy pronouncement, "Madam, I'm Adam," and Napoleon's melancholy musing on pre-exile days, "Able was I ere I saw Elba." Then graduated to longer ones, like the telescoped history lesson, "A man, a plan, a canal—Panama!" His two favorites of all time are the culinary "Go hang a salami, I'm a lasagna hog" and the naughty "A slut nixes sex in Tulsa."

And now *bob, bob.*

The water splashes on his back, and he is feeling enlightened as he cogitates:

Bob (Thomson)
Bob (Richardson)
BB (Billy Buckner)
Walter Retlaw
SS (Solomon Stein)

All palindromes from his visits to the past. All the same backward and forward. *Backward and forward*. Just like his trips through time, his round-trips through time, his shuttling from present to past and back again. Reminding him once again of Kierkegaard's aphorism regarding History:

Life must be lived forward, but it can only be understood backward.

Seth hops out of the shower, and it occurs to him that his age—33—also happens to be a palindrome. Not to mention Wally's apartment number—303. But enough already! He dries himself, gets dressed for his class with the bushy-tailed ones. It is nearly one thirty, and he's gotta skedaddle.

Just as he is putting on his Red Sox cap, he has the granddaddy of all epiphanies. What if . . . What if Papa Sol is, really and truly . . . *still alive*? Dear God. Why didn't this occur to him with such searing clarity before now? Did he just come to accept the fact that his grandfather had died after these past two years? Or was the idea of Sol's being taken by an old Yankee Stadium sweeper to a tiny apartment in the Bronx, with possibly irreversible amnesia, as witnessed during a possibly real trip to the past, just too preposterous for him to believe completely, deep down?

Clinging to his nascent hope, encouraged by his epiphanies of the meaning of Papa Sol's note and the twelve letters and all the prima facie evidence and now the palindromes, and buoyed by the increasingly strong belief—backed up by a trusting Kate—that his trips to the past *must* have been real, Seth, Hamlet-like, at long last springs into action.

"Hi. Is this four-one-one? Yes, Bronx, New York City. Do you have a listing for a Walter or a Wally Retlaw? That's r-e-t-l-a-w. On the Grand Concourse."

Seth waits for thirty seconds, then: "You don't? Are you sure? Well, could you please check again?"

Same story.

Beads of sweat form on Seth's forehead. "Well, thanks, anyway," he says and hangs up. So near and yet so far. Just like his grandfather, here he was, with his high hopes, only to be disappointed. Then, an idea, and he redials Information.

"Yes, can you give me a number for the missing persons bureau of the borough of the Bronx, in New York City?"

Seth writes down the number and thanks the operator.

He dials the MPB and finally gets a human being on the other end.

He tells the lady Wally Retlaw's name. He gives her the address on the Grand Concourse, plus Apartment 303. He says that his grandfather might be living with Wally and describes precisely what Papa Sol looked like last time he saw him, during the trip back to 2004. Then he waits.

And waits.

When the lady comes back to the phone, she says that yes, there is in fact a person named Wally Retlaw still living on the Grand Concourse and yes, there's a person living with him who fits his description of Solomon Stein and yes, Wally did contact the Bureau about two years ago but no, Mr. Stein had no ID and no one ever answered the notice or called the MPB and by all means, here's Mr. Retlaw's unlisted phone number and the best of luck to you and your grandfather.

"Thank you *so* much. You don't know what this means to me. I really, really appreciate your help. Bye now."

Land O'Goshen!

Seth dials up Wally, and his fingers are trembling so badly, he doesn't think he'll make it through the eleven numbers. Maybe Wally's not home? Maybe the nice lady was wrong, and Papa Sol is no longer there? Maybe something happened—

"Hello?"

"Hello, am I speaking to Wally Retlaw?"

"This is he. And who might this be?"

"Well, it's a long story, Wally, but I'll get right to the point. My name is Seth Stein. Is there a man with a beard who's about five-nine and seventy-eight years old living with you?"

"Yep, been a close friend of mine for two years now. Why do you ask?"

"Well, his name is Solomon Stein—I call him Papa Sol—and he's my grandfather. He's been missing for two years, and—"

"Now, how do I know you're his grandson?" Wally says protectively.

"Um . . . I guess you don't for sure, but please believe me, I *am*."

"But even if you are, how did you know he's living with me?"

"Okay, Wally. This may sound crazy, but please hear me out. I know you may not believe me, but this is the God's honest truth. I . . . I was given this very special baseball by my Papa Sol and it took me back in time to a few historical ball games and no one could see or hear me and I was at that Game 7 in Yankee Stadium, where you found him in a daze after everyone had gone, and then I followed you both back to your apartment and saw you take care of him—"

"But that's *ridiculous*. You traveled back in time? No one could see or hear you? You entered my apartment? What do you take me for, a—"

"Wally, please believe me. I was there. And, anyway, listen to me, how else would I know that his wound was on the right side of his forehead and it was swollen and a little purple around the edges and there was a single trickle of blood running down his cheek and you wiped it clean and you asked him if he had a wallet and he said no and you said you didn't live far and on your bed there's a blue plaid comforter and on the wall in your living room there are pictures of Satchel and Josh and Cool Papa—"

"So his name's Solomon Stein?" Wally says, relenting. "Always wondered what his real name was. I been calling him Josh, after Josh Gibson. Also wondered whether he had a family—"

"Listen, Wally, I'd really like to thank you for taking care of my Papa Sol all this time and for being his friend. It means an awful lot to me."

"Yes indeedy, my pleasure entirely. We had ourselves some good times, I can tell you. And he's been the best darn Yankee Stadium assistant I ever had. Now, I'm guessing you'd like to have your Papa Sol back real soon, right?"

"You took the words right out of my mouth, Wally. His wife, Elsie, misses him terribly, as you can imagine. And so do I. And his great-grandson, Sammy, too."

"Well, son, where do you live?"

"Cambridge, Massachusetts."

"Tell you what I'm gonna do. First thing tomorrow morning, Josh, er, Papa Sol and I are gonna get in my car and drive up to Cambridge, Massachusetts, and I'm gonna deposit him right at your doorstep, I am. I know how big this moment will be for you all, so I'll just drop him off, knock on the door, and be on my merry way. But you can be sure that I'm not planning to be a stranger and that I'll be coming up to Cambridge to visit him probably more often than you'd like."

"That's very kind, Wally. Know that you will always be welcome in my home."

"There's just one thing I should tell you about Josh, I mean Papa Sol—"

"What's that, Wally?"

"Seems he doesn't remember anything meaningful about his past, so be prepared. I know he loves baseball, I can see it in his eyes, but whenever I start to talk about the old days, he doesn't seem to recall any of the players. Must've been that bump on the head—"

"Yes, I know about that. I was really hoping he'd start remembering about his past by now, but truthfully? We'll all be thrilled just to get him back the way he is."

Thank God for kind and loving people like Wally in this world, Seth is thinking as he says good-bye and thanks again to the compassionate Yankee Stadium sweeper.

◖◗

Elsie Stein and Sammy Stein and Seth Stein and Kate Stein-to-be are waiting in the living room of the grizzled, gray-shingled Stein residence for the Big Moment. On the walls are signs with brightly colored writing that the whole family helped to create:

WELCOME HOME, PAPA SOL!!!
WE LOVE YOU, PAPA SOL!!!!
PAPA SOL, YOU'RE OUR HERO!!!!!

Kate is nervous, mostly for Seth, and Seth and Sammy are nervous, mostly for Elsie, and Elsie is beside herself with excitement and emotion and can hardly hold back the tears.

Small talk among the four is stopped dead in its tracks by the long-awaited knock.

Seth opens the door, and there he is.

Papa Sol.

Solomon Stein stands at the threshold between stoop and vestibule, at the threshold between a life without a family and one with.

To the relief of all, he appears not to have changed much physically since his last sighting in the fall of 2004, although a few more gray hairs and wrinkles have insinuated themselves on his head and face.

There Papa Sol stands at this double threshold, a faint smile gracing his lips, and it is clear that he has just returned from a grand adventure. Not unlike certain heroes of literature, like Odysseus and David Copperfield and Dorothy Gale, Solomon Stein—heroic and long-suffering—has been on a tortuous journey and has endured hardships and obstacles and has returned home to comfort and love.

He does not seem to recognize any of his loved ones, but despite his affliction, he is still a profoundly sensitive man, and everyone in the living room can feel that he appreciates the warm reception and is aware of the affection permeating the house and senses that he is surrounded by people who surely and most obviously love him deeply.

Papa Sol reciprocates the reception with the sweetest of smiles.

Grandma Elsie is the first to break the ice. She approaches her husband of sixty years and throws her arms around him in a wild embrace, her tears drenching the lapel of his jacket. Papa Sol is bewildered at first, but his look is soon transformed into one of acknowledgment and appreciation and pleasure. He must be someone pretty important to this lovely woman to merit such a greeting.

"Sol, my *dahlink!* It's your Elsie, your sweetie pie! I've missed you so, my love!" she says, knowing full well that

Sol is not yet, and perhaps will never again be, the husband and lover and pal and companion he once was to her.

Sol retains his sweet smile, but Elsie knows what the deal is. Still, she is ecstatic to have him back once again.

Seth and Sammy and Kate take turns hugging, kissing, and squeezing the Guest of Honor. Papa Sol knows that he is appreciated and wanted and loved, whoever all these nice people are.

Seth takes Sammy aside and cradles his son's face between his two loving hands.

"Remember the 1980 U.S. Olympic hockey team?" he asks.

"Sure," Sammy answers, unsure of where this is leading.

"Well, remember what the announcer, Al Michaels, said at the end of the game, when they upset the Russians?"

"Do you believe in miracles?" Sammy answers in his little announcer's voice, proud of the sports trivia genetic material passed on from Papa Sol to Seth to him.

"Well, *do you?*" Seth asks. "Because if you don't, how in the world do you explain the fact that the Bosox won the Series two years ago and that Papa Sol just came back to life and that tomorrow morning I'm gonna call your mom and ask her if we can please be friends from now on?"

Sammy's face lights up with the broadest smile in the history of the universe. No words are necessary to express what he is feeling in his heart.

Looking across the living room at his Papa Sol, Seth can't help musing upon the quirkiness of life and all the wonderful and not-so-wonderful things that have befallen Solomon Stein, this remarkable yet flawed human being. He is pondering the trajectory of Sol's secret life: the Thomson Frustration and the Terry Fiasco and the Buckner Bungle and the amnesia and the ultimate inability to savor, at long last, the attainment of the Holy World Series Grail by his beloved Bosox. He is ruminating on Papa Sol's dark side, but also on the bright side of Sol, this amazing husband and father and grandfather and great-grandfather and person. How unfair that his life had to turn out like this. Yet as Papa Sol always told him, *per aspera ad astra*: You can never get to where you want to go without struggles and challenges. So despite the setbacks, there is always hope for a new beginning. That's the way the old Papa Sol would want it, and that's the way it will be.

And while the champagne is being uncorked and sipped and Papa Sol is feeling more comfortable with the situation and the conversation is warming up all around, Seth Stein has one final epiphany. For no apparent reason, the P.S. at the end of the note his grandfather left him emerges in his brain. As he sips his Korbel, he suddenly realizes that the letters *P.S.* stand not only for Post Scriptum, but also for . . . Papa Sol! So maybe the message ends not only with what will *I* do after the ball has performed its magic, but Papa Sol, what will become of *you*?

Seth looks across the room at Grandma Elfie, who has her arms wrapped around her husband. Solomon Stein is feeling the profound love of this woman he doesn't recognize.

Elsie smiles at Papa Sol and he smiles back at her and then the smile is passed along, like a sacred family love note, from Elsie to Kate to Sammy to Seth.

It is the best of times.

In the midst of the joy, Seth remembers something that Gordon had told him on the phone when he called for the medical advice. Something about how it is possible for a familiar visual object to have a positive affect on a person afflicted with retrograde amnesia.

Sanguine Seth knows just what to do and goes into his grandfather's den. Sitting on the large oak Solomon Stein desk is the old picture album of baseball cards that just last week Seth had returned to its original and rightful owner.

Emerging from the den, he brings the album over to his Papa Sol, who is now seated on the sofa.

Seth opens the album up to the baseball card of Alpha Brazle, whose secondhand face is wizened and sunken and tan, like a battered old catcher's mitt whose pocket has been broken in and darkened through countless innings of abuse.

"Now, Papa Sol, this is ol' Al Brazle," Seth says to his grandfather.

Elsie Stein and Sammy Stein and Kate Stein-to-be are watching the proceedings with great interest and find it touching to see Seth sharing old memories with Papa Sol.

Papa Sol studies the baseball card of Alpha Brazle, and suddenly an odd look comes over his face, not exactly odd but quizzical and almost enlightened.

He opens his mouth and gazes straight into Seth's eyes and tilts his head and flashes this great big toothy smile, which wrinkles up his entire face and puffs out his cheeks, a smile that is broad and warm and piercingly affectionate, and even a little reminiscent of the old Papa Sol.

And then, looking at Seth with the most beatific of looks, eyes glistening slightly, Solomon Stein utters one single word, one simple word, one word that suggests to Seth, Elsie, Sammy, and Kate that perhaps he is beginning to snap out of it, to make the first, hopeful step on his arduous journey toward recovering his memory and resuming the happy life he had shared with his adoring family before he involuntarily abandoned them two years ago.

The word is *Setharoo*.

ACKNOWLEDGMENTS

I don't even know where to begin to thank all the people who gave me strength and support and inspiration during the writing of *Once Upon a Fastball*.

Actually, I do. Thank you, baseball, America's endlessly fascinating and complex National Pastime. Since 1950, you have given me unspeakable pleasure and treasured memories. Special thanks to Sal Maglie, Dave Koslo (after whom my dog is named), Larry Jansen, Jim Hearn, Don Mueller, Monte Irvin, Whitey Lockman, Eddie Stanky, Bobby Thomson, Al Dark, Wes Westrum et al., the New York Giants for whom I rooted; to the San Francisco Giants and the Boston Red Sox, for whom I root; to the incomparable and infuriating (to us Giants fans) Jackie Robinson; to Willie Mays, the greatest baseball player who ever laced up spikes; and, last but not least, to ol' Alpha Brazle, Sibby Sisti, Sam Jethroe, Ned Garver, Johnny Wyrostek, Erv Palica, Herm Wehmeier, Bud Podbielan, Roy Smalley, Ferris Fain, and all my other tragically jettisoned baseball cards (thanks again, Mom!).

I would like to thank all the generous and exceptional people who went to bat for me by contributing such terrific blurbs for the book jacket.

Speaking of which, to Franco Accornero for designing another grand slam of a jacket, *mille grazie!*

Next, great thanks to the passionate, energetic, and amazing Meredith Geisler, my MVP (Most Valuable Publicist).

I am deeply grateful to the outstanding and supportive staff at Kensington who had a hand in the production, publication, and promulgation of this book for, once again, hitting it out of the park. And especially to my extraordinary editor and friend, Michaela Hamilton, for her uncanny ability to maintain a happy balance between reining in and giving free rein; for her gentleness, grace, erudition, and unwavering support; and for the wise guidance and helpful suggestions that she proffered as we trotted merrily around the bibliobases together.

Next in the batting order is my wonderful agent, Joëlle Delbourgo. If there is a better literary agent on the face of the earth, speak now, or forever hold your peace. Thanks once again, Joëlle, for your expertise, your intelligence, your sensitivity, your encouragement, and your friendship.

A great big tip of the cap to Alan Brown, my eminent and gifted cardiologist, for helping me, well, just to keep hanging around.

Thanks to the most loving, loyal team of friends a person could have: Mary and Lance Donaldson-Evans, Barbara and Frank Fleizach, Margaret and Leo Schwartz, Phyllis Clurman, Beth and Bill Jaquith, Mark Cripps, Paula and Kenny Horn, Lynne and Seymon Ostilly, Rachel and Rony Herz, Linda and Pete Haller, Anthony Caprio, Ellen and Jim Gertz, Val Light and Bob Joseph, Joanne and David Frantz, Meryl and Hugh Herbert-Burns, Elayne and Hank Gardstein, Judith and Frédéric Bluysen, Willard Spiegelman, David Lee Rubin, Shelley London, Bernice Bernhard, Mike Appelbaum, Ann and Nat Greenfield, Bonnie Gorfin, Elise

Goldman, and the Finkelstein Cousins (Ellen, Lee, Steven, and Eric).

During my life, I have had the great fortune to enjoy and benefit from the knowledge of and passion for the glorious game of baseball generously shared with me by the following devoted fanatics: Frank Fleizach, Ken Horn, Bill Jaquith, Jim Gertz, Budge Upton, David DeVries, Gert Cabaud, Marty Appel, David Harman, Ray Robinson, Harlow Parker, Morty Goldman, Mark Borteck, Jon Maksik, Lon Hanauer, Jon Plaut, Kevin O'Neill, Bob Pasotti, and Gil Feldman. Thank you, all, for your unfettered rabidity.

Special thanks, in memoriam, to Alan Gorfin, one of the truly good people in this world. Alan, you will always be in my Friends Hall of Fame.

I'd like to thank my children for continuing to make me a proud and loving daddy and granddaddy: Noah (and wife, Carol, and kids, Stephen and Gavon), Jenny (and husband, Eric), and Sarah. It's so gratifying to see you three happy, self-assured, and independent: I guess all those years of playing catch in the driveway finally paid off!

And now . . . batting cleanup (actually, I occasionally do the dishes) . . . number one . . . Susan Ellen Love. Thank you, sweetie pie, for being such a fantastic wife, for being my best friend and my constant source of inspiration, and for being there at every stage of the tortuous writing process— reading first drafts, dispensing sage advice and feedback, and, above all, keeping me sane and healthy and happy.